THE BILLIONAIRE'S BIRTHDAY SECRET

TEXAS BILLIONAIRES SERIES
BOOK 3

JO GRAFFORD

ISBN: 978-1-944794-79-8

GET A FREE BOOK!

Join my mailing list to be the first to know about new releases, freebies, special discounts, and Bonus Content. Plus, you get a FREE sweet romance book for signing up!

https://BookHip.com/JNNHTK

ACKNOWLEDGMENTS

Thank you so much to my faithful beta reader, Mahasani, and my amazing editor, Cathleen Weaver — both of whom are also very dear friends. And as always, I want to give a big happy shout out to my Cuppa Jo Readers on Facebook. Thank you for reading and loving my books!

CHAPTER 1: BUTTERFLIES

THEA

He's perfect!
Thea Ferrell was supposed to be sketching storyboards, not daydreaming about the swoony executive VP she'd met at a friend's wedding. As the celebrity hostess of the award-winning Texas Homestyle Show, she was in the middle of gearing up for their biggest episode of the season, the Christmas episode. It was a lot of fun, but it was also a massive amount of work — work that wasn't going to get done if she couldn't focus.

With a sigh, she stopped pedaling her white desk bike, which she'd wheeled into the center of the room earlier, and hopped off the seat. If she couldn't build storyboards while cycling, she'd just have to find another way to rediscover her inspiration. Fortunately, her office was built to maximize her creative flow.

The walls were a calming blue-gray. Well, one of the interior walls was, anyway. She was lucky enough to have a corner office on the twelfth floor of a high-rise in Corpus Christi, so she enjoyed the luxury of two whole walls of floor-to-ceiling windows. The Moroccan cherry hardwood floors gleamed with polish, and the glossy white plantation shutters were louvered half-open to bathe the room in the maximum amount of sunlight.

On one end of the room was a mod ivory sofa resting on a pale blue rug. She used it for meetings with clients, brainstorming sessions with her film team, and even took an occasional nap there. On the other end of the room, a short flight of stairs led to her glassed-in recording studio that overlooked the rest of her office. A white bannister separated the two workspaces. Beneath the rail was a series of built-in shelves, containing everything from beverage fridges to props storage.

The only thing her state-of-the art cinematic office most unfortunately didn't contain was a time machine to make the hours fly by quicker, because she had a date this evening — her first date after an entire six months of not dating, to be exact. So she had an extra swarm of butterflies in her stomach over the thought of seeing Ford Merritt again. They'd met in Fiji at her bestie's brother's wedding, been stranded in a storm shelter together for a few hours, and had discovered some real chemistry zinging between them.

Unfortunately, Ford lived in Dallas, so it was one of those long distance relationship thingys. The kind she'd sworn she'd never get suckered into again, because they never seemed to work out. At least not once in her adult life had they worked. The two she'd attempted had started off with a bang, were fun and mysterious for a few weeks, then just as quickly fizzled out. Her last epic fail in the romance department was exactly the reason she'd decided to take a break from dating. She hope-hope-hoped she wasn't making a mistake by ending her dating diet.

Fortunately, Ford was a pilot, so he was able to turn the six hours of drive time between them into an hour and twenty-five minutes of flight time. As a top sales executive for Gulfstream, the sky was his office. He literally traveled the globe to meet with clients and prospective clients.

She was super lucky that his schedule was taking him down to Cancun to meet with a mega resort owner over the weekend, because that made the dinner date they had planned right on his way.

A triple knock on her door alerted her to her assistant's presence on the other side. She reached up to tap on her earpiece. "Come in, Ollie."

The door pushed open. Her right-hand man and partner-in-everything-show-biz-related   breezed inside with an emerald green sequin shirt draped over one arm and a stack of folders clutched in the other. A fifty-ish or so man in a dignified gray plaid suit, he boasted a receding salt-and-pepper hairline that he swore made him look wiser. In her opinion, he was more than wise; he was indispensable.

Oliver Patrick was seriously a jack of all trades. He fielded her calls, maintained her schedule, and played gate guard for the revolving door of guests who found their way to her office each day. He also could organize a banquet for two hundred charity patrons as easily as he could pull together a small, intimate gathering. Oh, and he occasionally served as her makeup artist before she went on set — like the entire months of August and September when their regular makeup artist went on maternity leave.

"What's with all the sequins?" She quizzically eyed the size and cut of the button-up shirt, figuring it was for her.

He waved it airily. "I'd like you to try it on, so we can see how it's going to jive against the holiday backdrops that just got delivered."

He was referring, of course, to the theme of this year's special Christmas episode. They were calling it Cowboys & Christmas Lights, though they'd yet to zero in on the perfect Texan or ranch to feature.

She accepted the shirt with a groan, wishing she had more to show for the many hours she'd been glued to her computer screen for the last three days.

Ollie chuckled as he moved past her to drop the

stack of folders on the slightly canted-forward desk tray of her bike. "By that dismal sound, I take it you're still noodling your way through the applications for our main holiday feature."

"I am." She flipped a handful of her white-blonde hair over the shoulder of her lacy shell top. Her discarded navy blazer was hanging on the back of her bike chair. "It's not that we don't have some amazing applicants. I just haven't yet experienced that this-is-the-one feeling with any of them. I know you know what I mean."

He nodded. "Who are the top contenders so far?"

"Well..." She frowned at the shirt in her hands, wondering if he meant for her to try it on right now as opposed to later on. "There's a super cute barn that's been converted to a veterinarian office up in Hereford. Then there's this scrumptious farmhouse just north of Houston that another family has renovated into a gift boutique. I'd like for you to contact them both and offer them regular features in January or February."

"Consider it done."

"However, I'd like to hold out a little longer for someone or something wildly extraordinary for our Christmas show." She waved her arms dramatically, nearly forgetting the shirt in her hand until one of the sequined sleeves narrowly missed slapping her on the nose.

She lowered the shirt to her side to fix her assistant with an imploring look. "Something that practically shouts hope, joy, and love." The only problem with holding out much longer was how quickly their November 1 deadline was approaching. It could take weeks to iron out all the logistics for a feature this size. Waiting so long to make a decision was going to leave them with nearly zero wiggle room for contingencies.

Ollie eyed her with genuine concern. "Are you one hundred percent sure we're still talking about the show?"

She wrinkled her nose at him. "Of course I'm talking about the show! What else would we be talking about?"

"Oh, I don't know." He lifted his brows and treated her to a comical look. "Maybe that dinner date I'm not supposed to know anything about?" At her gasp, he gave a knowing chuckle. "If you think for one second I don't know what it means when you color-block a dinner engagement on your calendar in your favorite shade of pink..."

"Fine!" she snapped, feeling a blush stain her cheeks. "You've unraveled one of my deepest, darkest secrets." *Big deal.* "But, no. My date has nothing to do with my decision on the Christmas feature." *Or does it?* Ollie's cross-examination was suddenly making her second-guess herself. *Is Ford Merritt the real reason I can't seem to think straight this afternoon?* She'd made very little progress on her storyboards.

"Okay." Her assistant cocked his head at her. Then he held out a hand. "The shirt will be perfect on you. You can hand it back now."

"But I haven't even tried it on yet," she protested.

"No need." His mouth quirked with humor. "You've brandished it in the air so many times in the past five minutes that I already got the visual I needed."

Relinquishing the lovely green shirt to him, she scrambled to put better legs on her thoughts for the upcoming holiday feature. "Don't get me wrong, I don't mind featuring family-owned businesses and all the typical outlets that make Texas, well...Texas." Plus, it greatly helped small business owners boost their visibility and increase their bottom line. "In fact, I love doing it. Heck, those shows are our bread and butter. For Christmas, though, I was hoping for..." She shook her head. "I don't know. Something less commercial in nature, maybe?" Preferably something that completely embodied the spirit of the holidays.

He grinned. "I was kinda hoping you'd say that." He angled his head at her desk. "Because something interesting arrived in the mail today that I'd like you to take a look at."

"What?" Her interest piqued. Most of the applications for their Christmas show had arrived via their online portal, but they'd left the option open for mail-in forms. Had Ollie single-handedly solved her current dilemma? It wouldn't be the first time.

He waved a hand toward the folders on her desk. "It's some artwork from a kid, actually." His voice sounded vague.

Okay. Maybe he hadn't yet saved the day, but there was still time. "Alright. Thanks." Her interest dwindled. She was forever receiving fan mail and gifts, including solicitations like these — people of all ages who fancied themselves to be the next darling of cinema. Future set designers and such. They sent her everything from personal sketches to digital files. This one sounded more like crayons. *Cute.* But not exactly what she was looking for.

He smiled. "Maybe sometime this weekend you could humor the kid and take a look at them?"

"Sure. No problem." She'd already moved to the sofa and was kicking off her orange, four-inch heels and replacing them with a pair of ballet flats.

"Well, I'll be around." He backed toward the door. "Call me if anything comes up." It was kind of a private joke between them. Ollie was always around. He ate, drank, and slept the Texas Home-style Show. He literally kept an emergency cot folded beneath his desk for all-nighters. The show was his life.

"'Night, Ollie." She hoped he remembered to

eat. Sometimes he got so busy working on sets and stuff that he skipped meals.

She heard the door click shut behind him while she was snatching up her briefcase. She was halfway across the room, heading for the exit when she remembered the folders he'd left on her desk. Spinning around in her flats, she returned to her desk to snatch them up and stuff them in the outer pocket of her favorite Italian leather case.

Time to get ready for my date! She'd waited all day for this. No, she'd waited all month, if she was being honest with herself. Maybe Ollie was right. Maybe her upcoming dinner with Ford was the honest-to-gosh real reason for her spike in jumpiness and disjointed focus.

All she knew was that she'd been crazy out of sorts ever since the trip to Fiji last month. She'd been trying to convince herself it wasn't because she was envious of her best friends, Eloise Cantona and Elon Carnegie. But, yeah. She was at least a little jealous of them. The three of them had been close since high school, but Eloise and Elon had always shared an extra special bond that all too often made her feel like a third wheel. After some friendly interference on her part, they'd finally admitted that special bond was love.

And now that they were dating, she was alone. Again. Just like she was back in foster care. One of the few kids that had attended their college preparatory high school without a big family name and pedigree to back her. The charity case on scholarship. Sure, Eloise and Elon had ended up offering her their hallowed uptown friendship (and heaven knew it had opened some pretty big doors for her, professionally speaking), but she remained an outsider, nonetheless.

A twenty-eight-year-old with no family and no roots. A woman who'd hired an administrative assistant in his fifties, simply because he might be the closest thing she'd ever get to a father figure in her life. She didn't even have a steady boyfriend. She never seemed to get far enough in her romantic relationships to be able to call a guy that.

Which was probably why she was so uptight about her upcoming dinner date. Every time she went out with a new guy, she hoped against hope that she might finally experience a spark of whatever it was that Eloise and Elon had. And she always went home disappointed.

But there had been some real chemistry between her and Ford Merritt. Maybe it was the sound of the water lapping the beach in Fiji. Or the electricity of the storm that had forced them into a shelter for a few hours. Or the moonlight the following evening. All she knew was that she'd enjoyed his company — a lot — and was really looking forward to seeing him again.

Like her office, the apartment she rented was on

the beach. The two buildings were only a few blocks apart, which was why she'd changed into ballet flats. She preferred to walk the short distance instead of driving her own car or hailing a cab.

Ollie fussed at her for traveling so much on foot, telling her it was unsafe for a celebrity show hostess to be alone on the streets like that. He was probably right, but so far she'd never run into any problems. Then again, she was careful — always wearing big, dark sunglasses and tying an enormous scarf over her hair. It was the one time of day she could be a part of a crowd. To blend in. To belong.

And tonight did not disappoint. The sidewalks alongside the city buildings were crammed with pedestrians. Many of them were strolling hand-in-hand or moving in small clusters, part of the Friday night dinner crowd.

The October evening boasted only the lightest of breezes, not quite warm and not quite cold. The perfect in-between weather before the bitter chill of winter blasted its way up the coastline.

She reached the front entrance of the Ocean Bay Resort and scanned her member badge to get the revolving glass doors moving. To her delight, one of the four sets of elevator doors was already open and waiting for her in the wide entry gallery.

Guess it's my lucky day! Hurrying to hop inside, she allowed herself the luxury of lounging back against the wall for a few moments. The glassed-in compartment started to move upward, giving her a panoramic view of the beach. The sun was a red and gold ball on the horizon, casting a rosy glow over the bay. Artwork in motion — the one and only reason she so willingly paid to live in an overpriced down-town suite.

It was truly a killer view — one she would've traded in a heartbeat, however, for the greeting kiss of an adoring husband or the happy chatter of chil-dren's voices upon her arrival. Instead, she sauntered alone down the hallway, turned her key in the lock, and stepped inside an utterly silent home.

Bolting the door behind her, she tossed her key on the entry table in the foyer. *I really need to adopt a puppy or a kitten.* She'd debated her options a thou-sand times but always put it off. It seemed cruel to adopt an animal, just to leave them alone all day long, five days per week. And sometimes on the weekends when she had to travel out of town to film her shows. *Maybe someday.*

She headed straight across her cozy living room to her bedroom, anxious to shower off the stress of the week. Tonight she was determined to take a break from work, a real break, and just enjoy living. Tomorrow she could get back to reading proposals for her show. Maybe the perfect application would just float down from the sky, so to speak, and land in her lap like an early Christmas gift.

Maybe it was because the holidays were so firmly

stamped on her mind, but she ended up discarding her original idea of donning a black cocktail dress in lieu of unveiling an all-new one that she'd been saving. She'd purchased it, thinking she might wear it to this year's company Christmas party, but tonight seemed like the right time to debut it.

The berry colored velvet settled over her feminine curves with a subtle snake print that seemed to glimmer in the light as she moved. Though the dress had long sleeves, it had a shorter skirt, which accentuated her toned legs. Her waistline was cinched in with a flattering knot detail. She completed the ensemble with a pair of velvet black heels that were held in place with a thin ankle strap, and a black beaded clutch.

A quick glance at the clock on the marble vanity made her abandon the idea of an up-do. She was running out of time before Ford's expected arrival. Not to mention, sometimes *less was more,* as the French liked to say. With that in mind, she left her hair down in its natural waves and popped in a set of black, princess-cut diamond earrings. They glinted alluringly from their white gold settings, simple yet sophisticated.

I'm ready. She gave herself one last once-over in the mirror to make sure she hadn't forgotten something major. Like her head. Then the doorbell rang, claiming her attention.

Pressing a hand to her heart, she willed her

breathing to remain normal as she traversed the apartment to examine the security code she'd assigned to grant her date entry to the fifth floor. Yep, it was the right one. She clicked the button on her wall panel to accept it. In less than a minute, a knock sounded on her door. She turned the knob, and there he was — the guy she'd been daydreaming about almost non-stop for five straight weeks.

Ford looked every inch the successful executive vice president of sales that he was. He was the epitome of casual elegance in a well-tailored black suit, a pristine white shirt that was unbuttoned at the collar, and no tie. His dark hair waved back from his high forehead, and his slate-gray eyes seemed to be drinking her in the same way she was drinking him in.

"Hello, you." He gave her a slight head-shake. "Since it's our first official date stateside, I know I'm supposed to say something poetic or eloquent about how beautiful you look tonight." He gestured at her with one hand, treating her to a flash of a silver cuff link. His half-smile was unabashedly admiring, shy even. "Which you do. But I hope you'll forgive me for skipping straight to the part about how glad I am to see you."

Um, wow! "Thank you." She felt her lips curve upward, reveling in the way his gaze caressed her. It was the kind of look that made her feel beautiful, no trite compliments required. "I've been looking forward to seeing you again, too." Despite the evening shadow darkening his chin, or maybe because of it, he was even better looking than she remembered. How was that even possible?

He rocked back on his heels and gave a short, self-deprecatory chuckle. "More than anything, I'm glad to discover you're real." He held out his hand to her. "That I didn't just dream up the fact that Thea Ferrell — *the* Thea Ferrell of the widely acclaimed Texas Homestyle Show — actually agreed to go out with me tonight."

"Oh, stop already," she scoffed, stepping into the hallway and pulling the door shut behind her. She gave the knob an experimental twist to ensure she'd remembered to lock it. She had.

He didn't back up as expected to make more room for her, though, so her steps brought them nearly toe-to-toe. Close enough for her to catch a whiff of his clean, sandalwood aftershave.

"So are you a dinner-first or a dessert-first kind of girl?" His rich baritone resounded through her, underscoring just how close they were standing.

She wasn't certain she succeeded in stifling a delicious shiver of awareness. "How about you surprise me?"

"Okay." He closed the short remaining distance between them and lowered his head. Then his mouth brushed against hers in the tenderest of kisses.

CHAPTER 2: SECRETS

FORD

Maybe Ford was losing his mind. Or at least his touch with the ladies. Because kissing his date at the start of the evening was not something he normally did. In fact, he could count on one hand the number of times he'd done anything so brash — all of never.

He was careful to keep his hands at his sides, not wanting to move too quickly with Thea. The way her soft lips moved against his was encouraging, though. It wasn't just wishful thinking. She was kissing him back!

He could have stood there all night, reveling in her warmth and sweetness. But he raised his head and took a half step back, instantly missing her touch. He had to work to keep his breathing at a normal cadence. "I'd say you're solidly in the dessert-first category."

"Looks can be deceiving," she retorted in a teasing voice that held a breathless edge. "I can't think of even one time I've ordered dessert before dinner."

He winked at her. "Glad I played it safe, then, and ordered dinner." He ushered her toward the elevators. "After you."

She breezed past him down the beautifully furnished hallway. A cozy lounge area had been set up across from the elevators, complete with elegant armchairs and a coffee table strewn with an assortment of books.

He quickly moved forward to reach around her when she started to press the button for the elevator heading down. "We're going up, beautiful."

"Really?" Her surprised blue gaze clashed with his.

"All the way to the rooftop," he affirmed, carefully watching her reaction.

She wrinkled her nose at him. "Though I'm sure the view of the bay is awesome from up there, it happens to be located in the high-rent district."

High rent, eh? That was funny. "Nah, I'm pretty sure the best view is right here on the fifth floor." He was pleased by her blush, though he was still amused by her humorous summation of the privately owned penthouse suites above them.

"I mean, it's not open to the public."

"True, but I happen to be friends with the new

owner." Her expression registered surprise, indicating she'd not heard about the recent acquisition of
her resort community by Cantona Enterprises.

She shot him an incredulous look. "You know
someone who just happened to move to the top floor
of my building?"

"Actually, I'm referring to the guy who owns
the entire complex, Roman Cantona." Not just the
one building. He owned all five of the high-rise
structures that made up the Ocean Bay Resort.
Ford was surprised the guy's sister, Eloise, hadn't
mentioned it. Weren't she and Thea supposed to be
close?

"Oh." She made a face. "Now that you mention
it, I think Eloise did say something about it a while
back. Cantona Enterprises owns a significant amount
of real estate in Corpus Christi these days. They're
always expanding. I don't even try to keep up with
all of their holdings."

They exited the glassed-in elevator and traded
their   one-sided   view   for   a   spectacular
360-degree one.

Thea blinked in astonishment at the lantern-lit
courtyard. His borrowed white 'copter was resting on
the helipad on the east side, and a table for two had
been set up on the west side next to a private lap
pool. Dwarf palms in urns anchored the four corners,
turning the rooftop into a tropical paradise.

"I was right." To his amusement, Thea spun in a

slow circle, soaking in the gorgeous evening. "The views are spectacular up here."

"From my perspective, they are." He couldn't seem to take his eyes off of her.

She spun back in his direction and colored prettily at the compliment. "Thank you."

"You're welcome." He pulled out one of the chairs for her to take her seat.

As previously arranged, their ghostly wait staff appeared and moved noiselessly to and from the table to serve frosted, crystal-stemmed tumblers of berry water. Next, a waiter sailed into their midst with two gorgeous cobb salads that were double drizzled with a creamy white dressing and a tangy vinaigrette. A stringed quartet secreted behind the greenery struck up a light, lilting number.

"This is delicious," his date sighed, closing her eyes momentarily over a bite of the salad the way he'd seen other women react to dessert. "I got so busy earlier today that I skipped lunch."

Aww, too bad. He was glad to be the bearer of sustenance and hoped she enjoyed the entrees he'd selected that were still forthcoming. "Tell me about your job." He leaned forward, his heartbeat accelerating over how breathtakingly lovely she was — and not just the skin-deep kind of lovely. Just like their first encounter in Fiji, she impressed him as being one of those rare, kindhearted, and truly decent people. "I intended to watch an entire season of your show before tonight, in the hopes of impressing you, but sorry. Time just didn't allow it." He gestured with his fork. "So if you don't find my honesty too off-putting, I'd like to hear all about your job, please." He wanted to hear all about *her*. Period.

"Ooo, you obviously didn't receive the warning memo." She made a face at him. "I've been told on a number of occasions that I have a habit of getting carried away when I talk shop. Maybe you should choose a different topic."

"Nope." He shook his head, grinning. "I must have missed the memo, so if you're in the mood to humor me..." He inclined his head conversationally.

"Don't say I didn't warn you."

"I won't."

Their gazes clashed and held for a breathless moment.

Then she gave a modest shrug. "I showcase homes and businesses in Texas. Everything from clever renovations to one-of-a-kind intrastate products and services. The whole idea is to give our viewers a taste of what it's like to live here in cowboy country." Her smile widened. "Emphasis on country."

He nodded. "Lots of boots and horses on your show, eh?"

"For sure. Plus ranches, rodeos, grill outs, 4H events, races, and county fairs. Right now, we're gearing up for our annual Christmas episode."

He could tell by the animation in her movements and the way her blue eyes sparkled, that she loved what she did for a living. "Sounds interesting. I take it your Christmas episode is a little different from the rest of the season?"

"It's supposed to be." She gave a gusty sigh and laid down her fork. "Normally, the right feature just falls into my lap, but this year..." She met his gaze with a rueful expression riding her classically oval features. "I'm having trouble, Ford."

Mirroring her movements, he laid down his fork at the genuine distress in her voice. He liked how she'd addressed him directly, without even seeming to realize it. "What sort of trouble?" Though they were about to discuss something that she clearly considered problematic, he was finding her musical alto to be both soothing and enchanting. The stress of his week was quickly vanishing beneath the spell of her presence. Call him an old-fashioned fool, but this was all he'd ever wanted. Someone like her to come home to in the evenings. Someone like her to talk to like this. Not just tonight, but every night.

For an answer, Thea made a moue with her pink petal lips, making him long to kiss her again. "So far, nothing that has crossed my desk feels right. Sure, I can showcase yet another house or barn. You can't go wrong with the way they're all jazzed up for the holidays. But, to me, that's just more of the same. We already have those kinds of features lined up for the entire month of December. What's more, every one of them is sharing a percentage of profits with our outreach project, exceeding last year's donations by two hundred percent. Wham, bam! Mission accomplished." She sighed again. "So I don't know why I'm crabbing about anything. Maybe I'm being unreasonable, but my gut keeps telling me we should gear the Christmas episode toward something...more." She raised and lowered her shoulders. "I just don't know exactly what that is, yet. I've been toying with ideas for weeks, and I got nothing."

Without thinking, he reached out to touch the top of her hand. "I may not know much about show business, but something tells me that the right opportunity will find its way to you. Just be patient." That's how stuff like that worked.

"Thank you." The worried creases on her peachy cream forehead relaxed momentarily. "And that's not entirely true about your experience with show business. Unlike you, I *did* take the time to watch your hot self strut your stuff in that Gulfstream commercial before dinner tonight."

"I did not strut!" A laugh rumbled deep in his chest. She was such a trip.

"Oh, maybe it was more of a swagger." Her gaze glinted wickedly.

He rolled his eyes, feeling his face grow red. "I can't believe we're having this conversation."

"Oh, really? Because the tens of thousands of

times it's been shared on social media and the millions of views it's received, tells me there are a whole lot of other women out there who would agree with me."

"Just stop!"

"Make me." She jutted her lovely chin at him.

Okay, maybe it wouldn't be all candles and roses to come home to a woman like Thea every night. Apparently, it would also be tongue-in-cheek insults and miles of sass.

"I have a better idea." He pushed back his chair, walked around the table, and held out his hand to her. "How about I treat you to an up-close demonstration of my famous moves?" Trying not to laugh, he signaled behind his back for the hidden quartet to strike a livelier tune.

"You're on." She allowed him to spin her into a dance. They dipped and swayed to the music. "Yeah," she sighed dreamily when he twirled her close again, "I'm pretty sure it's a swagger."

"Are we seriously still stuck on that topic?" he growled.

When she nodded laughingly, he swooped in to seal his mouth over hers. "There are other ways to end this conversation," he notified her between kisses.

She leaned back in his arms, flushed and amused. "Oh, this conversation is far from over, mister."

He caught the finger she waved under his nose and lifted it to his lips as the musical piece drew to a close. They stood there in the center of the courtyard a few moments longer, swaying gently back and forth in each other's arms. "Maybe it's a little early in the evening to bring it up, but I'm really hoping for a repeat of tonight in the near future." He already wanted to date her again. And again and again.

"It depends," she announced in a lofty voice, slipping from his embrace.

"On what?" He followed her back to the table to hold out her chair.

"Lots of things." She picked up her linen napkin and laid it across her gorgeous knees. "How well you feed me, for one thing. I'm famished," she confessed.

"Then let the feasting begin." He took his seat across from her and signaled for the waiter to serve their main course. After taking mental notes about her eating habits in Fiji, he'd been careful to keep things light on tonight's menu. Although she wasn't a full-blown vegan, she was undeniably a health nut. A celery crunching, morning runner kind of gal.

He watched her face light up when the blackened salmon fillets arrived to their table. They were lightly spritzed with lemon sauce and accompanied by a swirl of spiralized zucchini noodles, spaghetti squash, and carrot lace.

"This is amazing," she murmured, making an appreciative humming sound.

"I passed the test, huh?" *Score!*

"One of them," she retorted loftily. "There are still closets to be scoured for skeletons, that sort of thing."

Skeletons. Yeah, that was a topic he wasn't exactly looking forward to. He waggled his eyebrows at her to stall for time. "You first."

"I spent most of my childhood in foster care," she returned promptly, steadily meeting his gaze. "But I managed to get scooped up by a distant cousin with guardianship papers by the time I started high school. She wasn't very well off, but she helped me apply for a scholarship to attend the poshest high school in town. That's where I met Eloise and Elon. I'll probably never be able to prove it, but I suspect the Cantona and Carnegie families had something to do with my subsequent college scholarship, as well as the recommendation for my television internship that led me to where I am now."

Ford reached for her hand as she spoke, greatly touched that she was being so transparent about her past. And the way she so generously attributed her success to the help she'd received from others. It was modesty at its finest, because she was a shining light in her own right in the world of show business. He was even more thrilled about the fact she felt comfortable enough around him to confide something so personal.

"No doubt others had their input," he declared

softly. "But when I look at you, I see an all-around, self-made woman. You've worked hard. You've earned this."

"I'd like to think so. Turns out elbow grease laced with God's grace is a powerful combination." She frowned. "Guess I was determined to defy the statistics."

He raised his brows, not sure what she was talking about.

"The experts say that my background exponentially increases the likelihood I will suffer from homelessness, unemployment, or incarceration as an adult — three bullets I've managed to dodge so far. Probably because I was fortunate to have the right people come into my life at just the right times. Otherwise," she made a rueful face, "who knows where I might have ended up?"

And there was the modesty again. "I, for one, am very glad you ended up exactly where you are." He squeezed her hand.

"Me, too." She offered him a tremulous smile.

"I hope you additionally decide that I'm one of those right people who's come into your life," he continued.

She dropped her gaze shyly. When she looked up again, her smile had turned teasing. She slid her hand from beneath his to fork another bite of her fillet. "Time will tell, Mr. Tall, Dark and Mysterious. Okay, it's your turn to reveal a skeleton."

Great...not! "We-e-e-ll..." She'd been completely honest with him about a very sensitive topic. His gut told him that he was going to have to be equally honest if he wanted to move forward with their relationship.

She chuckled. "You're actually squirming over there."

You bet I am, and for one very good reason. He drew a deep breath. "I've been married before."

She grew still. "It doesn't sound like it ended well."

"It didn't. She was involved in a tragic car accident."

"Oh, Ford!" she gasped. "I'm so sorry."

But, wait. There's more. "It happened a few days after she left me. We hadn't yet gotten around to filing for a proper divorce." Nor had there been time to attempt a reconciliation. Or say goodbye. She was just gone.

"That's awful," Thea murmured. "And wildly unfair that you never got the chance to try to work things out."

Truer words were never spoken. As painful as their separation had been, that wasn't even the worst of what had happened during that sordidly dark time in his life. However, Ford wasn't quite ready to tell all. Not tonight, anyway. He could only hope the unearthing of one skeleton would satisfy Thea's curiosity for now.

THEA WAS a little surprised by Ford's confession. She'd not pegged him for a divorcee, much less a widower. However, she could tell by the shuttered look that came over his face that he was finished talking about his past. For now.

She was kind of hating herself for bringing up what had turned out to be such a depressing conversation. "Gosh!" She stuck her tongue out at him, hoping to lighten the mood. "Who came up with the completely horrible idea of dragging out skeletons, anyway?"

"Hey." He laced his fingers loosely through hers on the tabletop. "This stuff was bound to come up between us over time. I actually don't mind getting some of my secrets out of the way early."

Only some of them? "Oh, sheesh! There's more?" she teased, wondering if he'd meant to say that. Regardless, she agreed. She still cringed sometimes over the number of guys in the past who'd pursued her because of her looks and celebrity status — right up to discovering her lack of family name and pedigree — at which point they couldn't hightail it fast enough.

One guy, in particular, had done a real number on her heart. He'd been ready to go ring shopping before his wealthy family had pulled him aside and talked some "sense" into him. He'd moved up to become the president of the television station she now worked for, while she'd blossomed right where she was. However, she'd gained one very important take-away from their failed relationship: There was simply no point in emotionally investing in a relationship that wasn't going anywhere.

"I might have a few more secrets," Ford Merritt drawled with a faint twinkle in his eyes. "But I'd rather not scare you off completely by spilling all of them in one evening." He held her gaze intently, as if silently begging her to trust him.

So he had secrets. Well, she had one or two more of her own that she had no interest in revealing tonight, either. She studied his expression, unable to imagine him capable of doing anything that would make her run. From their first encounter, she'd sensed an ironclad brand of integrity in him. Plus, he'd been so up-front about so many other critical issues this evening, that she had no reason to believe he was holding anything back that would derail their relationship later on. He'd been a perfect gentleman with her, and a very romantic one, at that.

Thea studied their joined hands. "And if I were to tell you that I don't scare easily?"

He caught his breath at her words, and his shoulders relaxed as if a huge weight had been lifted from them. Then he raised her hand to his lips. "I'm happy to hear it." He kissed her fingers. "Any interest in taking a starlight tour of the city?" He angled his head toward the helicopter.

Her heart leaped at the romantic sound of it. "That's yours?"

"No. I borrowed it from a friend. My own bird happens to be parked at home in Dallas."

She gave a disbelieving laugh. "So do you ever drive anywhere? You know, in vehicles with four wheels?"

"Only when I have to." He stood and tugged her to her feet. "Given the choice, I'd much rather be in the air."

"I'm starting to see that." She walked hand-in-hand with him to the helicopter. Minutes later, they were soaring over Corpus Christi. He'd been right about the stars, too. They were popped out like a thousand white diamonds against a velvet black sky. After pointing out the bird's-eye view of various key locations around the city, he next flew her over the bay.

While hovering above the waves, he caught her eye and leaned in for a very tender, very thorough kiss that majorly intensified the magic of the night. He didn't speak again until they returned to the helipad on top of her apartment building. As the rumble of the engines faded, he reached for her hand.

"I meant what I said about wanting to see you again, Thea."

"I want to see you again, too," she declared softly.

"I hate the fact that there are 400 miles between us."

"Fortunately, one of us is a pilot." When he didn't answer, she hastened to add, "but that doesn't mean I can't hop on a flight now and then in your direction."

He leaned closer to brush his lips against her temple. "I don't mind flying down here. I just wish I could make it more often."

"What's your schedule like next weekend?" she asked hopefully, then immediately wished she could retract the question and blast all memory of it into oblivion. She didn't want to sound desperate.

"Can't." He toyed with her fingers. "But I'm available the weekend after that."

"Works for me." She swallowed a sigh. Two weeks felt like a million years away.

He grimaced as he watched her expression. "Wish we didn't have to wait so long."

"Maybe we don't." Emboldened by his words, she blurted, "Our office in Dallas has been twisting my arm about coming to meet with them between now and Christmas. Maybe we could squeeze in a lunch or dinner date mid-week."

He was silent for a moment. "I'd like that," he finally returned, though she sensed a note of reserve in his response. "A lot."

Hmm, it sure doesn't sound like it. "Well, it's just

a possibility. I have no idea yet if it will work out." She started to withdraw her hand, but he curled his fingers more tightly around hers and hung on.

"I really hope you can make it."

She didn't know what else to say, so she remained silent.

He lifted her down from the helicopter, and they found the rest of her meal from earlier packaged and tied with a ribbon. There was also a delectable slice of cheesecake piled with strawberries beneath a clear plastic dome lid.

"Wow! Thank you." She glanced wistfully around the courtyard. "For everything." It had been, hands down, the most romantic date of her life, complete with dinner, dancing, and a bird's-eye tour of the city.

"May I walk you to your door?"

She nodded, sad that their amazing date was coming to an end. The short ride down in the elevator was spent in charged silence. She watched the sparkling cityscape rise as they descended, wishing she could think of something light and clever to say. Normally, she was far more chatty.

Once they arrived at her door, she swiftly unlocked it so she could stow the food boxes on her hall table. Then she turned around in the open doorway to face him.

From Ford's shuttered expression, she wondered if she'd made a terrible misstep, such as giving him the impression that she was going to invite him inside. As a rule, she never did that with her dates. Like, *ever!* For all the obvious reasons. She wasn't that kind of girl.

"Thank you again for such an amazing evening." She hoped he heard the dismissive ring in her voice. *Time to go. Sorry.*

"'Til next time," he answered simply. Bending his head over hers, he gave her a light peck on the lips. Then he was gone.

Omigosh! She stared blindly after him. Then she shut the door and leaned against it, pressing both hands to her chest. *Omigosh!*

She'd just gone on a date with the talented, successful, wildly wealthy Ford Merritt. One of Elon Carnegie's closest friends. A guy right smack in the 1% club that she'd never be a member of, no matter how many times her fans voted her show to the top of the charts. The sudden desire to confide in someone had her digging her cell phone out of her clutch. She dialed her best friend, who conveniently happened to be Elon's fiancee, though she swore to herself it was a bestie call not a digging-for-info call.

Eloise picked up on the second ring. "How did it go?"

Thea loved how they could practically read each other's thoughts. "It was pretty amazing." She bolted the door, then glided in a daze to her living room sofa.

"Tell me!"

So she did.

"I didn't know he was married before," Eloise mused in puzzlement. "Then again, I only met him recently. He and Elon go way back, so he probably knows."

"Do you mind asking him about it?" Okay, so it was turning into a digging-for-info call, after all. *Nobody's perfect.*

"Oo, checking up on your new boyfriend, huh?" her friend chuckled.

"Something like that."

"Why? Are you worried about him?"

"No," Thea sighed. *Not exactly.* "Maybe."

"Okay. I'll see what I can find out. Anything in particular you want to know?"

"Everything," Thea chuckled ruefully.

"You betcha, sweetie."

"He's a man of many secrets."

"Well, we're going to uncover every one of them."

CHAPTER 3: BEST GIFTS COME IN SMALL PACKAGES

THEA

Thea changed into a pair of black yoga pants and a pink tank top. Though it was getting late, she felt nowhere close to sleepy. She wandered into her kitchenette to brew a mug of hot tea. Moving to the sliding glass door in her living room, she gazed over the bay while sipping in quiet contemplation.

Ford was out there over the water right now, flying in the direction of Cancun. She sent up a silent prayer for his safety. He was an experienced pilot, but it felt right, somehow, to add him to her prayers this evening. She doubted he would mind.

He was quickly becoming very special to her. So special, in fact, that she was already starting to wonder if there was any room in his professional, jet-setting lifestyle for a second marriage. Would he ever be the kind of guy who wanted a wife to come home

to again, or had he already gotten his fill of the ol'
ball and chain?

Maybe something Eloise found out from Elon
would shed some light on what had gone wrong
between him and his first wife. Maybe there was a
good reason for...

Her phone rang in the distance, making her
realize she must have left it on her nightstand.
Setting her tea on the bar, she quickly padded back
to her bedroom. Knowing it was probably Eloise, she
took a flying leap into her bed, snatched up the
phone, and prepared to listen to her friend spill all.

Her bounce onto the mattress had the unfortu-
nate effect of knocking over her briefcase she'd
forgotten was sitting on the corner of her bed. It
dropped to the floor, spilling its contents. *Great!* She
grimaced, knowing she'd have to retrieve all the
folders and scattered papers before falling asleep.
Otherwise, she'd likely go skating on a stray sheet in
the middle of the night when she got up for a bath-
room break.

But Eloise's private investigating work came first.

"Hello, darling." She leaned back against the
headboard. "I presume you're calling with an update
on Operation Boyfriend Secrets?"

"Am I ever!"

"Oh?" That sounded promising. Thea wiggled to
get more comfortable against the enormous pile of
white ruffled throw pillows.

"They were married eight years ago. He was only twenty-two at the time, just finishing up his degree at the Air Force Academy."

"Wait." Thea sat up. "He was in the military?"

"Aeronautical Engineering major. Graduated with honors and married his high school sweetheart the same day. She was a horse jockey, of all things. A rising rodeo star."

Thea made a face and sank back against the pillows. "Those don't sound like two careers that would mesh very well."

"They didn't. According to Elon, it was a problem for them from day one. They spent more time apart than together, and she put a lot of pressure on him to leave the military."

"Guess she succeeded."

"Well, that's the strange part. Ultimately, she's the one who pulled up roots. Quit her job a few months into their marriage and joined him at his first duty station in California. Elon said he kind of lost touch with them for a couple of years after that. Next thing he heard, they were separated. Before he had a chance to reach out and see what was going on, though, she was involved in a tragic pileup. They had her funeral in Dallas, since that's where her family was from. Elon flew up there to attend it."

"And?" Thea pressed when Eloise fell silent.

"Well, this is where his story gets even stranger. Ford was understandably a wreck at the funeral, so they didn't talk much. It was a small graveside affair. Family and close friends only. Closed casket. A very brief obituary in the newspaper. Soon afterward, Ford left the military and moved to Dallas."

"To be near his ex-wife's family?" Thea cried, wondering if she was hearing right. That hardly made any sense.

"Well, technically, they never got divorced, but I hear what you're saying. Told you it was strange."

"So then he put his aeronautical smarts to work for Gulfstream?" she mused.

"And has been with them ever since. Elon says he moved up the chain pretty quickly. He's one of their top VPs."

"Well, okay, then." Thea hardly knew what to think. Though Eloise had fleshed out a few details, she'd revealed nothing new. She mulled over Ford's claim that he still had a few more skeletons in the closet — ones he didn't want to haul out too quickly out of fear of scaring her away. At first she thought he might be kidding, but now she was pretty sure he wasn't. Moving to be near his in-laws sort of underscored that point. So what was he hiding in Dallas that even his closest friends didn't seem to know about?

"Just be careful, sweetie." Eloise's voice was sympathetic.

"I always am," Thea assured with more confidence than she felt.

"He seems like such a great guy, and Elon swears he's solid, but..."

"But." Thea repeated with a sigh. *Big but.*

"But you seem to be the first serious girlfriend he's had in years, and I don't want to see you get hurt."

First serious girlfriend. "Thank you." Her heart initially swelled at her friend's words, then sank at the note of caution in her voice. Was there more to the story than Eloise was telling her?

"It's just that Elon and I were the ones who introduced you to him, so we kind of feel responsible."

"It's okay. I've got my big girl britches pulled up." *I hope.* Her heart was feeling a little raw after all she'd just learned about the man she was dating.

"I know, Thea, but you also have a heart of gold — one that's already been through enough. I swear if that guy mishandles your sweet self in any way, I will personally strangle the breath right out of him."

"Ouch!"

"I mean it, sweetie!"

"Should I warn him?" Thea chuckled.

"That's your first thought?" Eloise exploded. "Fear for his safety? Gosh, you've got it pretty bad for the guy."

"I do," she confessed, and there was the root of the problem. "It wasn't supposed to happen this fast," she wailed, "but I'm pretty sure I'm falling for him."

"I can tell," her friend groaned. "Hey, do you want me to come over there tomorrow? I can bring ice cream, sprinkle, hugs, and a truckload of sympathy."

"Yes, please," Thea choked. "All the above."

"Oh, honey!" Eloise waited a beat. "Would you rather me come over there tonight?"

Thea's phone vibrated with an incoming text. She held it away from her ear for a second to see who it was from. The sight of Ford Merritt's name made her heart race. It was from *him*.

"No, that's okay," she said quickly. "At least one of us should get some sleep. That way you'll be bubbling with wisdom and advice when you arrive to scrape my sorry self off the floor."

"Oh, honey!" her friend sighed again.

"Bring chocolate syrup, please." Thea gave a damp chuckle.

"Consider it done. Carmel syrup, too. Promise!"

"Love you to the moon and back."

"Sending air hugs that I promise to follow up with real ones tomorrow."

The moment Thea disconnected the line, she tapped her phone screen to open Ford's message.

Had the best time tonight. Missing you already.

"Oh-h-h-h-h!" *So did I!* She hugged her phone to her chest, reliving the highlights of their amazing date all over again. Every time he'd held her, she'd felt cherished and safe. Every time he'd kissed her, she'd never wanted him to stop. But now that he was miles away, soaring high above the ocean, doubts were zinging at her from every direction. Doubts about his past. Doubts about what had gone wrong between him and his late wife. Doubts about his reasons for moving to Dallas. Doubts about dating a guy she had so many doubts about...

In extreme agitation, she threw her legs over the side of the bed, with the intention of going to brew herself a fresh mug of tea. Her toe landed on a sheet of paper instead of the rug. *Right*. In the nick of time, she remembered the spilled contents of her briefcase and was able to avoid skidding across the room. She gingerly stepped around the mess and squatted to gather it up.

The first sheet of paper caught her by surprise with its bright splashes of blues and reds.

What in the world? She snatched it up and frowned at it thoughtfully. It was a photocopy of a painting. A caption was engraved on a gold plate affixed to the lower side of its frame. It read, *My Texas Home*.

The painting was one of a small girl with long, dark-red hair flying behind her in the wind as she rode a pony in full gallop across a field. She was wearing a wispy white nightgown and was riding without a saddle in her bare feet. It was such a carefree painting that all Thea could do was stare in growing fascination. The artist had rather expertly captured the wild and free spirit of the youthful rider. He or she had also beautifully captured the wind in the girl's hair, as well as the leaves, which looked as if they were being ripped right off the trees.

At first, she assumed it was an autumn painting. However, a closer look revealed a farmhouse in the distance with a wreath on the front door. Nope. It was Christmas time.

Her heartbeat quickened as she reached for the next sheet of paper on the floor. It was another photocopy of a painting depicting the same girl. In this one, she was swinging from a trapeze in a gym. The background was dissonant and blurred, which meant the artist intended for the viewer to focus on the little girl. However, Thea could make out the faint glint of mirrors on a distant wall. Just like in the painting of the pony ride, the girl's hair was flying behind her in the air. The result was the same feeling of exuberant, unfettered freedom. This one was titled, *My Texas Dream.*

There were half a dozen other paintings, all labeled in a similar manner — *My Texas Peace, Hope, Joy, Love, Heart, and Victory.*

By now, Thea was dying to know the name of the artist. She hurriedly finished collecting the contents spilling from her folders onto the floor. Then she propped her briefcase upright against the foot of the bed and plopped back on her mattress. Spreading the sheets of paper across her bed, she found herself staring down at eight different paintings. The final two pieces of paper were a print-out of the two-page application to the Texas Homestyle Show.

The name of the applicant practically leaped off the page at her. *Paisley Merritt*. What a coincidence. Her mouth went dry. What were the odds of having someone apply for a feature on her show, who just happened to share the same last name as the man she was dating?

She scanned the rest of the application, her eyes gobbling up the paragraphs that were typed in the essay section. It read more like a letter.

Dear Miss Ferrell, I'm Paisley's grandmother, Tonna Riley. I hope you don't mind that I'm completing this application on her behalf, because she's only six-years-old. However, I think you'll find her artwork well worth your consideration, especially once you hear the many physical challenges she's had to overcome while learning to paint. She was born with a rare form of spastic cerebral palsy that has kept her imprisoned in a wheelchair her entire life. Although she may never walk or run, this sweet child rides horses and swings from trapezes every day in her paintings. She also dreams of starring in a movie someday, which is a little harder to depict in a paint-

ing, though I'm sure this amazing child will find a way.

In the meantime, I think you may be able to help make at least one of Paisley's dreams come true if you will consider featuring her on your Christmas show.

By now, tears were streaming so fast down Thea's face that it was difficult to keep reading. She allowed the application to fall to her lap, knowing with sudden certainty that she'd found the right topic at long last to feature on her show for the holidays.

Oh, Ollie! She wondered why he hadn't said anything. This was so clearly "the one" that there was no question in her mind about it. Wiping the dampness from her face with both hands, she drew a deep breath. A quick glance at the time told her it was way too late to call him to discuss it, so she texted him, instead.

You dirty dog! Holding out on me like that... We have the perfect feature in hand for our Christmas show!!!!!! Then again, you already knew that, didn't you?

Then she bent over the side of her bed to pull her laptop from her briefcase. Opening it and signing on, she did a search for all things Ford Merritt, and found what she was seeking in seconds. His late wife's obituary identified her as Tess (Riley) Merritt. The write-up was heavily truncated, only listing the barest of details concerning her memorial ceremony and interment. There were no "survived by" mentions, though she'd most certainly been survived by a spouse and parents. Nor any mention of the crippled infant she'd clearly left behind.

Thea's phone buzzed with another incoming message. Her heart leaped into her throat at the thought that Ford was writing her again. However, it was only Ollie responding to her dig from a few minutes ago.

Very down and very dirty, but I didn't want to spoil the surprise. Call me tomorrow, and we'll talk turkey about bringing the next Michelangelo to our studio.

Thea couldn't stop smiling. Even though it was close to midnight, it was as if the sun had been permanently turned on inside her. Featuring Paisley Merritt on the Texas Homestyle Show was going to amount to the most epic holiday feature she'd ever watched, and she was a television show junkie! Not only was the problem finally solved concerning who to feature on her Christmas episode, she'd also stumbled across Ford Merritt's deepest, most precious secret.

And it was thankfully one she could live with — no ice cream needed.

She should probably outright cancel her gal pal session with Eloise tomorrow. For one thing, she was no longer stressed out. For another thing, she was going to be way too busy putting her head together with Ollie's, getting the ball rolling on the logistics of their Christmas feature. Furthermore, she plain old wasn't ready to spill the beans on Ford's private life just yet. Not even to Eloise. What she'd discovered about him and his family this evening was his, and his only, to tell his friends when he was good and ready.

In the meantime, Thea could finish falling head over heels with him in the quietness of her own home.

Blinking back happy tears, she slid off her bed and returned to the kitchen to make that mug of tea she'd been craving. She chose peppermint tea this time, since she was in such a festive mood. Then she carried the mug and her phone to the oversized chaise lounge parked beside the sliding glass door overlooking her balcony. On a whim, she unlocked the door and cracked it open an inch before taking a seat — not enough to chill the room down with coastal breezes, but enough to hear the sound of the waves lapping the beach.

She enjoyed the scent of peppermint swirling upward. Never had a mug of tea tasted better, probably because this one was laced with the hope of a woman falling in love. Love for a man she was suddenly determined was going to become more than a boyfriend. And love for his daughter that she couldn't wait to meet. Her heart ached like crazy for the small child who probably had no memory of her mother.

Gosh, but Thea could certainly relate to *that*! Seconds later, her stomach was flooded with butterflies over how she was going to break the news to Ford that his daughter had been selected as the main feature for her Christmas show. Did he even know that Paisley and her grandmother had sent in an application?

Wow! So many details about Ford's background were starting to make sense now — why he'd left the military, why he'd moved back to Dallas, and why Elon and Eloise couldn't seem to pinpoint any details about him dating much since both of those events had occurred.

I volunteer myself! Thea was totally fine with the idea of being Ford's first serious girlfriend in years. She set down her mug of tea and opened up her messages on her cell phone. She was finally ready to text him back.

Miss you, too! Looking forward to seeing you again.

CHAPTER 4: OLD WOUNDS

FORD

During his four and a half hour flight to Cancun, Ford could think of little else besides his date with Thea. How much fun she was to visit with. How good it had felt to hold her in his arms when they danced together. How much she made his heart pound every time they kissed.

Which was actually quite a few times for their first official date. Then again, what did he know? It had been years since he'd dated. Despite how much effort he'd put into planning their dinner, he'd probably done just about everything in the wrong order — starting with kissing her the moment he'd arrived at her door.

He smiled at the memory. Then his smile grew wider at the fact that she hadn't seemed to mind. Nope. Not a bit. In fact, she'd kissed him back, which was making him feel a thousand shades of cocky right now. From their first encounter in Fiji at Roman Cantona's wedding, he'd wanted to date her. And now he was. And things were going well between them.

But they wouldn't be going well for long if he didn't come clean with the whole truth about his life. About his daughter and her special needs. About everything. If he'd learned anything at all from his failed marriage with Tess, it was that love could only be built on one hundred percent honesty.

That's where he and Tess had gone wrong. They hadn't worked out the issues concerning their different careers before marrying. They hadn't discussed the ins and outs of starting a family together. And neither of them had been ready to become parents when Paisley was conceived — much less the parents of a special needs child.

It made his insides turn cold all over again at how devastated Tess had been when she found out she was pregnant. To her, it was as good as watching her career pour down the drain. Her unplanned pregnancy had made it impossible to continue racing horses, per her doctor's orders.

Since Ford's jet was flying on automatic pilot, he reached up to clutch his head with both hands at the memory. At the time, he hadn't understood just how devastating it was for her to leave her horse racing days behind. He'd been too busy secretly rejoicing over the fact that they could finally be together. But that was before he understood that being together was never going to be enough for her. The afternoon she gave birth to their disabled child, he'd had to stand by helplessly and watch her finish shattering.

To this day, he wasn't convinced that her real intention was to leave him and their infant daughter for good. She'd just needed some space to deal with stuff. To absorb. To cope. But her tragic car accident had cut those efforts short, instantly turning him into a single dad. One without the first clue how to be a dad.

His phone buzzed with an incoming text message. He hoped it was from Thea. It was. He greedily devoured the words on the screen.

Miss you, too! Looking forward to seeing you again.

His heart raced at her response. He wanted so badly to dial her number just to hear her voice again, but it was getting late. Instead, he settled for sending her another message. If she was awake, she would receive it right away. If she was asleep, she could read it the first thing in the morning.

Can't stop thinking about kissing you.

Her next text came almost immediately.

I'm not exactly sleeping here, either.

He chuckled in exultation and started typing again. *Mind if I call you in the morning?*

Her response flashed back. *Do you really want to wait that long?*

He typed, *No, but I won't land for another two hours. I hope you're asleep by then.*

It only took a second or two for her to respond. *Wake me.*

Her words made his heart pound all over again. This was the kind of relationship he'd dreamed about having with Tess years ago. Loyalty. Commitment. Longing for each other when they were apart.

Maybe they'd been too young and too immature. Or maybe their feelings for each other simply hadn't run deep enough. After beating himself up for years over those questions, Ford was coming to the realization that he might not ever have the answers he was seeking.

But as of right now, in the middle of the night over the gulf waters, he was finally okay with that. Because of Thea Ferrell.

The last two hours of his trip couldn't go fast enough. He hit a smattering of rain during the last leg. It was accompanied by some medium-sized gusts of winds that made his Gulfstream shudder. The shaking and shuddering continued as he made his final descent, but he was able to nose her in for a smooth landing.

The runway was slick with rain as he shuttled his way toward the fixed based operations on the northwest end of the airfield. Crew members were waiting in neon vests and flashlights to guide him to his designated parking spot near the customs building. In the end, he waited until he made it through customs and taxied to the hotel before calling Thea.

Since it took a few rings for her to pick up, he figured she'd finally dozed off, and no wonder. It was past two in the morning.

"Hi, Ford." Her voice was slurred with sleepiness, yet it was the sweetest sound in the world to him.

"Hey, you."

"Did you make it to the hotel?"

"Yep." Her concern with his wellbeing warmed his heart. He kicked off his shoes and tossed his suit jacket across the chair beside his bed. Then he sank, fully dressed, against the headboard with a silent oof of satisfaction. It felt good to be horizontal again. "Sounds like you finally caught a few Z's."

"I may have chased a few down," she chuckled.

"Sorry if I woke you."

"I'm not. I'm glad you called."

"Me, too." He was grinning like an idiot as he closed his eyes, soaking up the sound of her voice.

"I'm glad you made it there alright."

Man, but he wanted to kiss her again! "Hey, can I ask you something?"

"Sure." Her voice went all soft and shy.

"I know we just started dating, but I'm ready to make it an exclusive thing." Apparently, sleep deprivation could make a person bold.

She chuckled again. "I'm ready for that, too."

His heart pounded harder. "Just to be clear, I'm asking you to be mine. To date me and only me."

"And I'm saying yes, so long as you're agreeing to the same terms."

"That I am. I'm a one-woman kinda man. Always have been, in case you're wondering."

"Not so much, since Eloise sorta let slip over the phone yesterday that you haven't had a serious girl-friend in a while."

"Ah. So you're talking about me behind my back, now, beautiful?" He'd seen for himself in Fiji how close she and Eloise were, so he was hoping that was a good sign.

"Just doing my homework," she shot back.

"And now I'm work."

"All men are work."

"Burn." He whistled softly.

"That didn't sound like a denial."

"That's because I'm not in the position to deliver the kind of comeback I want to right now."

"Oh, really?" She sounded breathless. "What kind of comeback is that?"

"The kind that doesn't involve talking."

She was silent for so long that he got a little nervous. "Am I putting you to sleep?"

"No," there was a bubble of laughter in her voice, "though I *am* dreaming."

"Of what?" *Please say me.*

"Of kissing you back."

Even better. "I'm okay with that. More than okay." He paused a few beats before adding, "Because in case you can't tell, I'm falling for you."

"You better be, since you just agreed to be my boyfriend."

"Your one and only boyfriend," he reminded in mock severity.

"Jealous already?" she teased.

"Of every guy who drools over my celebrity girl-friend on television, day in and day out? Heck, yeah."

"Says the hottie who starred in the world's most viral airline commercial."

He groaned. "The memes on that gig are killing me." *Truly killing me.* He was never going to live it down. When he'd agreed to his company's request to film the commercial, he thought he was crossing off a bucket-list item. *Chance to be on live T.V. Check!* But ever since then, he'd been getting hit on by perfect strangers all across social media. As in, thousands of women asking him out. Chat groups had formed among fans, who were rigidly divided between Team Pilot and Team Tarmac Dancer — the guy who'd totally cut up the pavement in the background of the commercial.

"In case you're wondering, I'm Team Pilot all the way," she cooed.

He groaned again. "I take it you've seen the chat groups."

"Full-fledged member, baby."

"Nooo!"

"I'm kidding."

"I sure hope so."

"Not about being Team Pilot, though. I'm solidly in his camp."

"Thanks, I think."

"So..." Her voice grew soft and shy again. "I'm happy to tell you that we finally ran across the perfect feature for our Christmas show."

"Happy to hear it, babe." And he was thrilled that she wanted to share it with him.

"It's completely different from anything we've ever filmed before, and I mean anything." The excitement in her voice was palpable.

"No kidding!" He settled more comfortably against the pillows, cradling the phone against his ear. "Is it a state secret or something you can talk about?"

"State secret, but since you're my boyfriend now, I'll trust you with it. But only after you cross your heart and promise to add a few extra kisses to our next necking session."

"I'm in!" he snapped so fast that they both started laughing.

"She's an absolutely precious, wildly talented, young artist."

"Aha. What are we talking here?" He grinned, thinking of another very precious, wildly talented artist who was very near and dear to his heart. "Play-dough sculptor? Expert sidewalk chalker?"

"More like the next Michelangelo. She's a painter. I'm talking child prodigy stuff. Her grand-mother was the one who sent in the application. I don't quite have all the details yet, but Ollie will probably reach out to them tomorrow to officially offer this sweet, beautiful baby the Christmas slot on our show."

Child prodigy? Grandmother? Sweet, beautiful baby? Ford felt the breath leave his chest. Then he started to sweat. Was it possible that, by some random wild-hair coincidence, Thea Ferrell had stumbled across his biggest, most protected secret? Then again, there was nothing in her words or tone to suggest that she had. Or at least no evidence that she'd connected the dots to him...yet. She sounded too casually animated. Too nonchalant. But, seri-ously! What were the odds that there was another child genius painter in Texas with a grandmother who worshipped the ground she walked on? He clenched his jaw. The moment he got off the phone with Thea, he was half tempted to make a second phone call to wake up another very important female in his life.

"Hello, hello! Are you still there, Vice President Merritt?"

He sat up in bed, wearily running a hand through his hair. "We need to talk, Thea." Even if she hadn't yet connected the dots, she would in the next twenty-four hours. He needed to come clean with her now, while he still had the chance.

"That's kind of what I'm trying to do."

"About this kid, I mean. What's her name, Thea? I think... there's a chance I know her." His mouth went dry.

"You think, huh?"

"Please, just..." *Tell me. I'm begging you.*

"It's Paisley. Your daughter."

A strangled sound wrenched from his chest. He nearly doubled over while trying to catch his breath.

"Are you okay, Ford?" Her voice was soft again, and a tad scared.

"I will be." He dragged in several bracing breaths of air, then shot to his feet. "When did you find out?"

"A couple of hours ago. Right about the time you sent me your first text."

He coughed. "So the whole time we've been talking here..."

"Was the sound of me *not* running and screaming from the last skeleton you were so reluctant to mention during our dinner date."

Tears burned his eyes. "Okay." He couldn't choke out more than those two syllables without starting to weep.

"As it turns out, I have another secret to share, too."

His brain was a big pile of mush. He cleared his

throat and said the same stupid thing again — the only thing he seemed to be capable of saying at the moment. "Okay."

"I love children, Ford."

"Well, this one's ah..." His voice broke. "Special."

"I know. If you'd like, I'll snap a picture of what her grandmother wrote on the application and email it to you right now."

"Yes, please. I'd like to see it," he rasped.

"Fair warning. It made me cry." She sniffled damply. "Then I had one of those epiphany moments and texted Ollie to tell him your precious child was *the one* we'd been holding out for. She's the message of hope that people so desperately need to hear this time of year, Ford. The kind of miracle who will inspire people to believe all over again." Her voice hitched. "But only if you give us your permission to have her on the show. We wouldn't do anything without your express approval. The signature-on-documents kind."

His phone vibrated with her incoming email, which he swiftly read while his ears were swimming with her kindhearted words about hope and miracles. He dragged in a heavy breath. "Thea, please tell me you understand that you're dating a guy with a daughter who's never going to leave her wheelchair." It was a big deal. He needed some acknowledgment that she recognized that fact — the fact that he didn't have the luxury of just thinking about himself, or even their relationship, for that matter. Someone else already had a very large claim on his time, attention, and emotional energy.

"Not true. I've seen the paintings, Ford. Or at least photocopies of them. She understands what it means to be free. More, I suspect, than most people I know with legs that work."

It was all he needed to hear. In her own unique way, Thea did understand. His shoulders shook as he started to weep silently.

"Ford, please, please, please assure me that you're okay!"

It was a while before he could regain command of his voice. "I'm okay if you're okay." *Holy smokes!* He hardly recognized the hoarse, scratchy voice as his own.

"Why wouldn't I be?" She sounded astonished.

"Hang on a sec." He strode across the room in search of a box of tissues. Laying down the phone, he blew his nose and quickly washed his hands. As he stared at himself in the mirror, a red-rimmed, haggard, sloppy-haired monster with a much-wrinkled dress shirt stared back. *Nice!* He was glad Thea wasn't present to witness this version of him.

Retrieving his phone, he marched back across the room to stare out the hotel window. The lights were off in his room, so he could see the twinkling spotlights of the few boats that were out on the water.

"Okay, I'm back."

"Missed you."

He smiled. *Man, I love you!* The thought nearly rocked him off his heels. "Missed you, too."

"You sure you're okay?"

"Like I said, I was more worried about your reaction than mine."

"That actually makes me sad."

"She didn't want her, Thea," he blurted, needing her to understand.

"Who? Oh-h-h..." she sighed, sounding heartbroken as his meaning sank in. "I'm so sorry, Ford."

"Yeah. Me, too." It was a huge comfort to finally unload the biggest burden of his adult years on her enormously empathetic ears.

"Any particular reason?"

"I have some ideas, but nothing concrete. We didn't get to work through anything before..."

"So I gathered."

"We were too young, I guess. Not ready for the real trials of life. Tess was already struggling with the idea of having to give up her career to follow the drum. Then she got hit upside the head with our unplanned pregnancy. Finding out Paisley was special was the final straw. It more or less broke her."

"I'm really sorry about your first wife, Ford." Thea's voice was cautious, as if she was carefully choosing her words. "It breaks my heart just thinking about all the things you've suffered. I'm not even going to pretend to understand, because I've never walked a day in your shoes." She drew a shuddery breath. "But I'll say this."

He leaned closer to the window to press his forehead to it, welcoming the cooler temperature on his aching head. "Uh-huh."

"I spent most of my childhood wishing on a star for a family. I was so starved for attention and affection that it probably warped me for life. So that's where I'm coming from when I say what I'm about to say next."

If Ford had been in the same room with her, he would have wrapped his arms around her and hugged her like he was never going to let her go. "I'm listening, babe." It was as if they'd suddenly switched roles, and now he was offering comfort to her.

"I would never, ever, ever, ever, ever, ever, *ever* walk away from my family if God was merciful enough to give me one. Not ever!"

Wow! He grinned, hardly able to believe he was having a conversation like this with the hot-as-firecrackers, platinum blonde, and divinely curvy celebrity hostess of the Texas Homestyle Show. "I love you, Thea Ferrell." He felt like weeping again.

"I love you, too, Ford."

He wanted to kiss her so badly that he could hardly stand it. Pressing a hand against the window, he stared down at the water. "Wish you were here with me in Cancun."

"So do I," she murmured.

"I'd take you walking on the beach tonight."

"Raincheck, please?" she chuckled.

"Count on it. I, ah..." His mind raced over his schedule for the upcoming week. "It wouldn't be for long, maybe only a couple of hours, but would you want me to swing through Corpus Christi on my way back to Dallas mid-day on Tuesday?"

"You seriously have to ask?"

"Just checking." If his grin grew any wider, it might crack his face.

"Consider mid-day Tuesday blocked off and completely reserved for you."

"I can't wait to see you again."

"Same."

"Okay, darling. I should probably let you get some sleep."

"Probably." But she didn't sound in any hurry to hang up.

"Dream about me, will you?"

"Trust me. The only guy haunting my dreams for weeks has been tall, dark, gray-eyed, and dancing across the tarmac in a Gulfstream commercial."

He barked out a laugh. "You're a truly horrible human being for bringing that up again."

"But you love me for it."

"More than I ever dreamed possible."

"Goodnight, Ford."

"'Night, babe."

He couldn't stop grinning the entire time he

showered and changed. Instead of rolling straight into bed, though, he first took a moment to kneel in front of the window. It was one of those enormous floor-to-ceiling resort windows, so he could see for miles even from his knees. As he stared at the vast wonder of the dark, wind-tossed seas, he whispered. "Thank you, God. Just...thank you."

CHAPTER 5: SHOW TIME

THEA

Though Thea had been up talking to Ford for at least an hour in the middle of the night, she rolled out of bed at the crack of six the following morning. Her body clock was accustomed to a certain schedule that was hard to break, even on the weekends. Oddly enough, she felt refreshed enough to hit the ground running. Literally.

Since it was cooler this time of day, she shrugged a zip-up sports jacket over her tank top and pulled on her tennis shoes. Twisting her hair in a ponytail and strapping her phone to her upper arm, she deemed herself ready to hit the beach.

There weren't too many beachcombers strolling around yet, so she nearly had the place to herself. It was one of her favorite times of day, before the rest of the world woke up. It was just her, the sound of the water, and God. Sometimes she listened to inspirational music while she ran. Other times, she preferred nothing more than the sound of the waves.

Like today.

Her lips moved in a silent prayer as she ran. *Thank you for bringing Ford into my life. Plus Eloise, Elon, Roman, and Ollie. And thank you for the precious little miracle girl I'm about to meet.*

She was so looking forward to meeting Paisley that she could hardly stand the wait. Throwing a glance at the horizon, she willed the sun to rise more quickly. Then she snorted out a laugh at her own ridiculousness.

After a four-mile run along the water's edge, she cooled down for a few minutes on the balcony outside her living room while sipping on a bottle of flavored water. Then she glanced at her phone. It was only going on seven-thirty. She burned another half hour of time by showering and dressing for the day. By eight o'clock, she couldn't help herself. She started texting.

Ford was first. *Morning, sunshine!* She attached a selfie of her leaning over the balcony to blow him a kiss.

He sent a selfie in return of him walking out on a pier to grab breakfast over the water. There was a picture of a crab on a sign in the background, presumably the restaurant he was heading to. He'd captioned it: *Being this far away from you makes me crab-by.*

She shot back. *A punster, huh? Now you tell me. Where was your warning label?*

His response came pretty quickly on the heels of the last one. *Consider yourself warned, beautiful. Times ten.*

She tapped out the cancellation for her ice cream date next and sent it to Eloise. *So sorry, but something has come up at work. Can we reschedule?*

Eloise shot back a meme of a cartoon stomping his foot. *Who's going to eat all this ice cream I bought? Six different flavors, dozens of toppings…*

Thea snorted out a laugh. *Okay, you had me going for a second, there.*

Eloise's retort flashed across the screen. *Good. I made you laugh. Mission accomplished.*

Lastly, Thea dialed Ollie. There was no way she could put everything she had to say to him in a mere text.

He picked up on the first ring. "How did you know I was even awake?"

She pretended innocence. "You sleep? I honestly wasn't aware of that fact."

"Very funny."

"Your ability to stay awake 24/7 is why you make the big bucks."

"Correction. That's why I'll be asking for a pay raise soon."

She shrugged. "We both know you're worth ten

times what the station pays you. I'll sign off on any amount you request and send it up the chain."

"Now that you mention it," he breezed, "there's actually something I want more than a raise."

"Talk to me, partner." She pulled out her mental notepad and pen. Ollie wasn't a whiner or a complainer. If he said he needed something, then he needed it. She'd pull whatever strings it took to make it happen, just like he always did for her.

"There's a rumor flying around that the station is trying to talk you into relocating to Dallas."

She scowled, knowing it was far from a new rumor. Their higher-ups had been dropping hints on the topic for two straight years. "Really? Who's saying that?" Had something new hit the gossip channel? If so, she hadn't heard it yet.

"Call it a hunch. All I'm asking is, when it happens, I want you to take me with you."

She wrinkled her nose at his unexpected request. "Weren't you born and raised in Corpus Christi?"

"You're the only one I'm going to work for," he returned flatly. "If you turn me down, I'll retire on a houseboat and become a professional drifter."

"Well, that would be a tragic loss. The world of show business would never recover."

"Exactly."

"But to be perfectly honest, Ollie, I have no plans in the works to relocate to Dallas."

"Yet."

"Do you know something I don't know?"

"I know you're dating a pilot who lives up that way, and you're about to feature his six-year-old daughter on our Christmas show. I might be pushing sixty, but I think I can connect those dots."

"Really? I didn't think you were a day over forty."

He snorted. "You're extraordinarily talented, my dear, but lying was never your strength."

"Fine. I'll keep my day job," she quipped.

"And me."

"And you." Wow! He wasn't giving up on the topic.

"Good. Now we can talk turkey." Without missing a beat, he jumped right into business. "I have the contract and necessary authorization forms ready to hand off to your boyfriend."

"Thanks. He's flying through town on Tuesday. He can sign everything over lunch." Her mind raced ahead to the next line item on her inner checklist. "I need your assistance with something else."

"Figured that. What's next, General Ferrell?"

They'd always worked together like this. She was the one on their team who spun the dreams. He was the guy who built the logistical legs and made them run.

"The kid wants to be a movie star, so let's create her perfect moment in the spotlight, starting with a trip to Dallas to interview her in her own environment. I'm going to need you to come with me for that."

"Glad to see you took my request seriously."

"And one of our camera guys."

"Done."

"As soon as possible after Tuesday."

"Roger that."

"My next request is going to require you to dust off your passport."

"Sounds interesting."

"It's also going to require you to convince Ford Merritt to fill out a future guest survey for Birthday Island."

"Isn't that the place in Fiji you visited a month or so ago?"

"Yes. His birthday is on the fifteenth of December, and I'd like to film our last segment of our Christmas show during it."

"So he's a billionaire, eh?" She could hear the curiosity and speculation in her assistant's voice.

"'Fraid so."

"Didn't say there was anything wrong with it, Cinderella."

She winced at the nickname. It was a little too on-the-nose. "I'm still absorbing the idea."

"He's not your ex, Thea."

"I know, Ollie, but—"

"He's not your ex," he repeated firmly.

"Thanks," she mumbled and ended the call. No,

Ford wasn't her ex, but he most unfortunately lived in the same city as her ex. If things continued in the direction they were going with Ford, and if Ollie was right about her ex renewing his offer to relocate her to the home office, well, that was one last skeleton she might have to drag out of the proverbial closet. The one skeleton she'd always hoped would stay buried.

THE NEXT FEW weeks passed in a whirl of preparations for the Christmas show. And the high-light of those weeks was every moment Thea got to spend with Ford and his daughter.

Her first appointment with Paisley was the Friday following Ford's signature on all the documents. He ignored her company's approval to fly her and Ollie to Dallas. Instead, he flew down to fetch them, himself. While Ollie napped in one of the recliners in the main cabin, Thea rode shotgun next to Ford.

At first, she sat stiffly in her seat.

After takeoff, he reached over to loosely weave his fingers through hers. "Penny for your thoughts?"

"I'm terrified," she confessed.

His high brow wrinkled with worry. "About meeting Paisley?"

"Of course not!" She shivered. "I just know I'm

not a real co-pilot. I don't want to bump any buttons and send us spiraling into the side of a mountain."

"Relax." His forehead smoothed. "I've probably spent more time in the air the past few years than I have on the ground. I'll get you there in one piece. Promise!"

"I trust you, Captain Merritt."

In the end, however, it wasn't her fear of the cockpit or even her first introduction to Paisley that proved to be the most stressful part of her day. It was the fact that Ashton Butler was sitting in the great room of Ford's mansion when they walked hand-in-hand through the arched doorway.

The president of 6Square Productions. The man who'd broken her heart six years earlier. Her notorious ex who'd dumped his poor television apprentice girlfriend before she became the high-profit, award-winning hostess of his top-viewed program, The Texas Homestyle Show.

"It's good to see you again, Thea." He stood when they entered, unfolding all six feet two inches of his rangy G.Q. frame from the ivory leather sofa. His half-smile had once melted her heart, but no longer. She knew it was as false as the six shades of straw highlights he paid to have dyed into his professionally tousled hair. Every detail of his appearance screamed big bucks, from his perfect manicure to his soulless dark gaze. When he looked at her, he didn't see a real woman; he saw an investment. A piece on his chessboard to be strategized the same as the stocks, bonds, futures, and commodities in his vast portfolios of investments.

Since she couldn't return his greeting without lying through her teeth, she nodded stiffly. "What are you doing here, Ashton?"

His smile turned chilly. "Same as you. I'm here to meet the star of our upcoming Christmas show."

But she knew it was more than that. He'd been avoiding the Corpus Christi office for years, more than likely so their paths would cross as little as possible. Which hardly explained his unannounced presence at the Merritt residence.

"I'm Ashton Butler." He moved across the round Persian rug to hold out a hand to Ford. "President and CEO of 6Square. No doubt Thea has already told you all about me."

Nope. Never mentioned you, jerk. Thea's stomach knotted at the thought that she'd be explaining why to Ford later on. Skeletons could be such a pain in the patoot sometimes.

"Ford Merritt," Ford answered easily. He had to drop Thea's hand momentarily to shake Ashton's. Then he splayed his fingers possessively across her lower back. "It's an honor to finally meet my girl-friend's boss."

Before the silence turned overly awkward, a middle-aged woman swept down a curved staircase into their midst. She was as slender as a pole in her champagne column dress, and her auburn hair was piled into an elegant knot on top of her head. "Miss Ferrell." She glided across the hardwood floor with both hands outstretched. "It is so wonderful to finally meet you. I'm Tonna Riley."

Thea shook her hand. "Thank you for sending me your granddaughter's application."

The woman's smile was warm and welcoming. "She's talked of little else since your assistant called us. She's been floating around here on the biggest cloud of excitement over the prospect of being on T.V. Speaking of which..." Her head swiveled in puzzlement. "Where is the little minx?"

A shiver of movement caught Thea's eye on the other side of the room.

"Daddy!" a girlish voice cried. "You're home!" A tiny girl in a tiny wheelchair rolled out from behind a massive two-story Christmas tree. The wheels were a blur as her chair flew across the room.

"Princess!" Ford stepped away from Thea just in time. The child launched herself from the chair like a miniature catapult and landed in his arms. He swung her around and around until she was giggling uncontrollably.

"I'm so dizzy, my head is about to fly off," she squealed. Her arms clung tightly to his neck.

"Oh, no!" he groaned in mock concern. "That would make a terrible mess in the living room, wouldn't it?"

"Nope!" she assured in a high-pitched, matter-of-fact tone. "Nanny Kate says there's absolutely nothing between my ears on painting days. That's why my math lesson wouldn't stick this morning." To make her point, she shook aside her hair to wiggle an earlobe at him.

Thea was utterly enchanted by the child's energy and wit. She was like a ball of sunshine. Happiness in motion. Nothing other than her wheelchair even remotely suggested she was an invalid.

Thea motioned behind her back to make sure Ollie had the camera guy in position. However, a glint of a lens from one of the overhead balconies alerted her to the fact that cameras were already in place and already rolling. It must have been Ashton's doing.

Hating the necessity of giving him any credit, she stiffly turned to catch his eye and gave him an approving nod. Thanks to him, they'd caught Paisley's flight across the room and her interaction with her father on film.

"I have someone I want you to meet, princess," Ford drawled. "Her name is Miss Thea Ferrell."

The child's expressive eyes widened as they settled on Thea. "You're the lady who's gonna put me on T.V."

"I am." She beamed a smile at her. "So long as your daddy agrees to let us film you."

"Oh, pu-lease, daddy!" Paisley Merritt implored,

clapping both tiny hands to her father's cheeks. "Please, please, please, please, pleeeeeeease say yes!"

He pretended to gravely consider her request, as if he hadn't already signed mountains of paperwork to approve it days ago. "Well?" He made a face at her. "Maybe you and I could negotiate an agreement that works for both of us."

"Anything," the little girl breathed with a maturity that belied her years. "I'll do anything, daddy!"

He pursed his lips and nodded. "For one thing, you'll have to start eating all of your vegetables on veggie night."

She gasped as if he'd stumbled across a terrible secret. "I already eat all the carrots, daddy."

"Yes, but you feed the peas to Pug under the table, don't you?"

She blushed and glanced away. "How did you find out?"

"Because I'm your dad, and dads know stuff."

"Oh." She chewed her lower lip as she mulled that over.

"And your head can't be empty during your math lessons. Not even on painting days."

She sniffed and curled her pert little nose in the air. "But my painting tutor says I need to clear my head of everything else and let the inspiration flo-o-o-w."

From the change in her accent when she said the

word *flow* while rippling her fingers in the air, it was clear she was repeating a rant from her tutor. It was so hilarious that everyone in the room burst out laughing. Even Ashton, who didn't normally do anything spontaneous.

Their delightful meeting with Paisley led to a tour of her painting studio on the third level. They took a mirrored elevator up, with the child chattering excitedly in her father's arms the entire way. Not surprisingly, Ford had devoted an entire room in his home to his daughter's art. There were framed prints lining the walls and three different easel stations. Shelves and tables brimmed with paints, brushes, daubing instruments, palettes, canvas boards of varying sizes, and other supplies.

Cameras rolled every step of the way. The many angles being filmed would make it easy later on for Thea to grab snippets of the most poignant and camera-worthy moments in Paisley's presence.

At one point, Ashton sidled up to her and bent his head to speak directly in her ear. "Ask her about the fabric hanging from the ceiling."

Thea despised the intimate way his breath warmed her lobe, but she couldn't fault his discretion in making the suggestion. Or the fact that he was allowing her to remain in full control as the hostess of the show.

Stifling a shiver, she gave him a jerky nod and waited until Paisley finished demonstrating one of the marvelous ways she painted verbs onto her canvas.

"You pretty much just have to keep everything floating in the same direction that the wind is blowing," she chuckled.

But Thea knew it was far from that simple. The child possessed a real gift for pressing oils to her canvas. Her tiny fingers seemed to fly over the painting as she brushed, daubed, and swabbed. A swish here, before her brush moved back to hover over her palette. *Dip*. A slash there before the next hover of her brush over her palette. *Dip, dip, dip*. A swift transfer of a dollop of white into the middle of her green to lighten the hue. *Dip, dip. Wide stir. Dip*. And voila! Different shades of leaves were born on the brown tree stump winding its way skyward.

Paisley's brush movements were so deliberate and graceful that they brought to mind the arc and sway of a dancer. Thinking of dancing made Thea glance away from the child to peer up at the red and green strips of fabric hanging from the ceiling. She'd originally presumed they were part of the holiday decor. But no. Ashton was correct. They were more than that. She squinted at the intricate twists of silk around a series of steel hooks and shells drilled into the ceiling. Unless she was mistaken, there were ball-bearing swivels between the hooks, though it was a little difficult to see from her vantage point below the twenty-foot ceilings.

She gave an experimental bounce on the floor and was surprised at how much buoyancy it possessed. *Yep.* This was more than a child-friendly rubber floor. It was specially poured, because they were standing in a studio that doubled as a gym.

Gliding across the room to stand directly beside Paisley, Thea was astonished to find her painting a bright slash of red amidst her forest of trees. As the red strip took shape, it became apparent that she was recreating the curve of the red fabric that was hanging directly in front of her easel.

"Tell me about the red in your painting, Paisley." Thea's gaze flitted briefly to Ashton's. "It's starting to look a lot like the red silk hanging from the ceiling here in your studio."

The child wiggled on her high-back stool. She was strapped into place on it with a seatbelt-type apparatus. "Oh, those are my aerial silks." She waved her brush off-handedly, narrowly missing painting a streak of red across Thea's white satin blouse.

"Tell me more," Thea pleaded in a soft, beseeching voice. "I want to know everything there is to know about how you make your beautiful art."

Paisley plunked her paintbrush in a glass bowl of water and pivoted with excitement in her seat. "It might be easier if I show you." Her gaze lifted to her father, who'd been standing silently next to her grandmother by the door all this time. "Please, daddy! May I do a few wraps?"

"Sure, princess." He beckoned for Thea to join him. "We'll need everyone to clear the center of the room and hug the walls, please." He leveled his gaze on Ashton. "Everyone, including those on the cameras."

Her boss nodded and motioned for the three camera guys to comply. They jogged to the outer perimeter and took new positions.

Thea joined Ford, who immediately drew an arm around her middle and tugged her against his side. He bent his head to whisper against her cheek. "I take it you and Ashton Butler have history, huh?"

She shook her head. "He's just a skeleton," she assured. As painful as it was, she would tell him as much as he wanted to know when they were alone again.

"I can live with that." He pressed his cheek to hers before lifting his head.

Low music filled the room from recessed speakers that Thea hadn't even noticed until now. The soft swell and hum of strings and horns wound around them like a melodic embrace. She instantly recognized the classic orchestral tune of Canon in D Major by Johann Pachelbel.

Then the occupants of the room gasped in unison as the tiny girl unbuckled herself from her chair and reached for the green silk behind her. She gracefully climbed the fabric nearly to the ceiling, using nothing but her arms.

"Oh!" Thea breathed, awe-struck by the incredible upper body strength it must have taken to complete such a feat.

The child launched into a graceful set of twirls, most of them involving various twists of the fabric around her delicate hands and tiny waist. At one point, she curled her body head over heels in a mid-air somersault.

Her audience started to clap. It soon became clear to Thea that this was how Ford's daughter had strengthened her fragile little body and learned to control the ofttimes uncontrollable movements of spastic cystic fibrosis.

Ford dipped his head next to Thea's once more. "She underwent a series of surgeries to relax the stiffness of her knee and ankle joints. She's also on a low dosage of some cutting edge medications specifically designed to help a child in her condition."

Thea felt her eyes grow damp. Though she nodded, she was unable to tear her gaze away from his miracle child. Only minutes ago, Paisley had been spinning magic with paint. Now, she was making art out of a thin strip of silk in the air.

Thea caught her breath again as the music crescendoed through its final stanzas. For a moment, she was petrified that Paisley was about to fall. But no. Her lithe little figure was simply rolling — rolling straight down the cascade of green emerald silk. Somehow the magical strip of fabric remained intricately intertwined around her waist and hands to propel her gracefully to the floor.

Or, rather, almost to the floor... At the last second, she arced her tiny frame and launched herself back onto her artist's stool in front of the easel. The orchestra struck an even livelier tune, as if celebrating her success. This time, Thea recognized the melody of one of Vivaldi's most famous concertos.

Hands clapped and cameras rolled while Paisley beamed at them like the exquisite little starlet that she was. She even waved and blew kisses.

"Oh, Ford!" Thea breathed, pressing both hands to her heart. "She's spectacular. An absolute miracle."

"Yes," he agreed softly. "So are you." His fingers gently brushed the dampness of tears from her cheeks. Then he tipped her face up to his and touched his mouth to hers.

Music and voices swirled around them like a happy cloud, and time stood still. When Ford lifted his head to gaze down at her, his face was brimming with love.

And then she knew.

I have a family now.

The room was already cleared out, making Thea wonder just how long she'd been held captive beneath Ford's spell. Ollie and the cameramen were gone. So were Tonna Riley and Ashton Butler.

Something told Thea that she hadn't seen the last of her ex, certainly not if a move to Dallas was in her future. However, she would cross that bridge when she came to it.

Paisley's childish babble reached her ears, reclaiming her attention. "Are you gonna be my new mama, Miss Thea?"

CHAPTER 6: THE DANCE
FORD

F ord spared the email from Elon Carnegie an eye roll. His friend had forwarded him the notorious survey from the Birthday Island resort. If he thought Ford was the kind of guy to spend scads of money on himself for his own birthday, he sure didn't know him very well. He almost deleted it before the final sentence caught his eye.

Ollie put me up to this, which means you're doing it for Thea — so be a good sport and fill it out, alright?

Making a face, he reluctantly scanned the questions. Three in particular made him smirk.

What do you do for fun?

I enjoy spoiling my daughter and girlfriend.

Does your perfect getaway involve sand

and sunshine, mountains and snow, or something else?

I'm   a   happy-wherever-Thea-Ferrell-is kind of guy.

Name the one person, place, or thing that never fails to make you happy.

Thea's arms!

Those weren't the answers he typed, of course, though he was highly tempted to. Instead, he suffered his way through the quirky survey, trying to give answers that Thea might find useful for whatever she had planned.

Guess this means we're heading back to Fiji. He didn't have a problem with that, so long as Thea was coming with him. His reservation at the birthday resort was confirmed within twenty-four hours, after which he authorized opening a tab with them. If it made Thea happy, he was more than willing to invest in an overpriced vacation.

However, nothing was charged to his account during the subsequent few days. *Interesting.* That wasn't normally how reservations worked, but okay. His few attempts to contact the resort resulted in an it's-okay-we've-got-everything-under-control   email. That was fine with him. He had more important things to worry about.

He squeezed in as many trips to Corpus Christi

as he could during the last two weeks remaining before his birthday trip. Plus, Thea made one more trip to his home to interview and film Paisley. His daughter was ecstatic to be receiving so much attention from the woman she was convinced was going to be her new mama.

As Ford was lounging in the doorway of Paisley's studio, studying the two females he adored most in the world, he felt the light press of Tonna Riley's hand on his shoulder.

"I've waited a long time for this, Ford," she declared quietly. She stood beside him, and together they watched Paisley merrily demonstrate to Thea how to paint a bird.

To watch a woman mother my daughter the way she deserves? He reached up to cover his mother-in-law's hand. *So have I.* "Thank you for being so supportive. I know this hasn't been easy for you." No doubt the idea of him moving on from her daughter had stirred untold amounts of grief. Her husband had passed shortly after they'd buried Tess, so it had been just the two of them for the past six years — a widowed grandmother and a single dad — raising Paisley the best they could between them.

"More like wonderful!" She sniffed in indignation. "Trust me. Seeing my favorite son-in-law happy again after all these years means the world to me." She continued in the same low alto, "And don't get me started on the marvelous change in Paisley. I don't think my granddaughter has stopped smiling since the day you brought Thea into her life."

"Neither have I," he confessed.

"I've noticed." She squeezed his shoulder again. "Just be happy, Ford."

"Yes, ma'am." Those were marching orders he was all too happy to follow.

"About that trip to Fiji you mentioned, I'm probably going to make myself scarce."

"Where will you go?" He glanced lazily over at her, having been fully expecting this conversation to arise.

"I was thinking of taking a long overdue trip to see my cousins in Florida."

"The ones you never talk to?" He arched his brows at her.

"Please don't make this any harder than it has to be, Ford. You and Thea need your space, and I don't see how the mother of your late wife is going to help—"

"Stay," he interrupted, pulling her hand from his shoulder. He drew an arm around her shoulders and hugged her against his side. He knew she needed assurance that she would continue to have a place in his and Paisley's lives. "We need you. We're always going to need you."

"What about—?"

"Thea's going to need you, too, Mother." He'd long since thought of her as such. With his own parents and grandparents hundreds of miles away in the Deep South, he'd needed her in recent years as much as she'd needed him. There was no way he was going to let one big blessing in his life edge out another.

"But, Ford," Tonna protested softly. "I always knew this day would come. "You don't need to—"

"Thea, darling." He raised his voice so it would reach across the room.

"Do you need something, babe?" She'd been so engrossed in her impromptu painting lesson from Paisley that she hadn't been paying them much attention until now.

"Sure do. I need you to convince Paisley's grand-mother that she is not the third wheel now that you've joined our inner circle."

Thea's lovely laugh bounced around them like a warm caress. "Technically, she's the fourth wheel, and I can't name one make or model of vehicle that runs better on three wheels instead of four. Can you?"

Tonna gave a huff of surprise. "A fourth wheel? I've been called a lot of things in my day, but that's a new one." Her perfectly painted lips widened into a grateful smile. She was wearing well-tailored black slacks today with a Christmas red blouse and gold ballet flats.

She was well put together as usual, every hair in place, making Ford wish she'd just relax and throw on a pair of jeans for once. She tried too hard. That was her problem. He always got the vague feeling she was struggling to make up for her daughter's absence, somehow. But what had gone wrong between him and Tess wasn't her fault or his. It had just happened.

Thea shrugged. "If you're still not convinced we need four wheels in our inner circle, then consider this." She angled her head speakingly at Paisley, who was humming beneath her breath as she painted. "There's no way a woman of your depth and compassion would, in good conscience, ever be able to walk away from this."

"You don't pull any punches, do you, Miss Ferrell?" Ford's mother-in-law stared thoughtfully at the woman he was falling more and more in love with each day.

"No. Life is too short, and family is too important." At Paisley's insistent tug on her arm, Thea's expression softened as she bent her head once more over the canvas.

"Oh, my lands!" Tonna Riley trilled softly for Ford's ears alone. "Don't you dare let this one go, son!"

Thea's gentle voice wafted their way. "Yes, sweetie. I see the cardinal you tried to hide in the tree."

Paisley giggled. "That was too easy. Maybe I should hide him better."

"No, way!" Thea protested. "Cardinals aren't meant to be hidden. They're colorful for a reason. Some little birds are meant to shine for all the world to see." She unconsciously bent closer to the child and kissed the top of her head.

Ford gave a satisfied huff. "I promise to never let her go," he assured the woman he was standing next to. "Inside my head, I'm already on my knees."

IN THE END, they took a decent-sized crowd on his jet to Fiji. Elon and Eloise joined them, with Elon riding co-pilot. Roman and Celine were more of a last-minute addition, but they showed up right before the plane took off and hopped aboard, waving their passports.

For reasons that no one seemed to be able to explain with any clarity, Paisley was also traveling with them to her loud and childish delight — which naturally necessitated a massive addition of luggage and supplies, as well as her grandmother and nanny.

Ollie and two cameramen made up the final three of their entourage. Their presence explained why he hadn't seen any charges yet on his tab at the birthday resort. Thea must have gotten the trip approved as a work expense, something that would've had to go through the approval of her higher-ups, i.e. Ashton Butler. Only time would tell if that was going to be a problem for him and Thea. She might consider Ashton to be nothing more than a skeleton, but his gut told him that the man wouldn't object too loudly to being elevated to something a little more than that.

Since Paisley's Christmas feature wasn't scheduled to air on the Texas Homestyle Show until the twentieth, Ford could additionally assume Thea's crew intended to film one last scene or two with his daughter in Fiji. The only detail he couldn't tie into that theory was his birthday celebration, which was scheduled to take place tomorrow evening.

But, again, no one seemed to be able to solve that mystery for him. Roman wandered his way to the cockpit a few hours into the trip and urged him to take a break. Since Ford hadn't enjoyed a single moment alone with Thea since the flight began, he sought her out.

And found her bent over her laptop in his private office in the rear of the cabin.

He propped his hand on the doorway. "Still working, I see."

She glanced up at the sound of his voice and caught her breath. Quickly shutting her computer, she stood and smoothed her hands down her creamy sweater and distressed jeans. "Hi! I didn't hear you come in. I'm just back here going over storyboards and editing videos."

She seemed a little nervous, idly toying with a

strand of hair before shoving it abruptly behind her ear.

"I can help with that." He strode in her direction.

"With what?" She watched him, mystified, as he rounded his desk and reached for her.

"This." He traced the shell of her ear that she'd flipped her hair behind, loving the way her expressive blue gaze locked on his. "And this." He bent to brush his mouth against hers.

"Ford," she sighed, wrapping her arms around his neck.

Yeah. She could forget whatever video editing she'd been working on, because he might not let her out of his arms until his break was over. He nipped a soft trail of kisses down her cheek and along her chin. "This is the best birthday I've ever had," he noted huskily.

"Au contraire. It's not until tomorrow." She tapped his nose teasingly. "We haven't even reached the island yet."

"Doesn't matter. I have you." He kissed her again. "All my wishes have already come true." Well, not quite all of them. He had one last plan to set into motion.

"It does matter, and I'll prove it to you tomorrow evening." Her smile held a hint of a challenge.

He cupped her face in his hands, enjoying her scent and nearness, as well as the sound of her voice.

"You still haven't told me if you're going to do any more filming with Paisley."

She made a face at him. "You must have been one of those kids who shook every present under the tree before Christmas morning," she accused.

"Guilty." He grinned.

"I knew it!" She shook a finger beneath his nose.

He swooped closer to kiss it. "I guess this means you're going to make me wait for my birthday gift?"

"Fo sho, Mr. Pilot, sir."

"Please tell me you have a plan to keep me distracted in the meantime," he teased.

"As a matter of fact..." She stretched on her tiptoes to press her mouth to his.

He closed his eyes as her warm lips and soft touch enveloped his senses.

"Is it working?" she whispered.

"Yes. Don't stop," he whispered back.

THEY ARRIVED in Fiji in the wee hours of the morning. Mandy, their faithful hostess whom Ford remembered from his last visit, met them with a clipboard in hand and a pair of black limousines idling behind her. She was the administrative assistant to the director of the resort, Mr. Green, and the glue that kept everything together on the island.

Under her direction, their sizable party was

transported to the main resort building. Everyone was dispersed to their respective rooms, presumably to catch up on some much-needed sleep.

Only Thea lingered in the hallway. "Happy birthday, Ford." She slid her arms around his middle and laid her head against his chest.

"Thank you for arranging this trip," he muttered, burying his face against her hair. "No one has ever gone to this much trouble for my birthday."

"Just wait until you receive my gift," she noted sleepily against the fabric of his shirt.

He hugged her closer. *Already have. I'm holding her right now.* He couldn't imagine her topping that.

"And until you do," she added in a mildly warning voice, "I'm going to need you to stay out of the ballroom."

"No problem." He toyed with a strand of her hair. "I'd rather take you out on the water, anyway."

"That's sounds amazing, but let's get some sleep first." She tipped her face up to his. "Kiss me goodnight."

"No can do, Miss Ferrell." He pointed at the sun pouring through the nearest windows. "But I'm happy to kiss you good morning. Or kiss you for no reason at all."

AFTER A FEW HOURS OF REST, she finally humored him and allowed him to take her out for a spin on one of the island's yachts. The water was crystal blue and clear as glass. They could see all the way to the shallow ocean floor in places. An idyllic couple of hours flew by way too quickly. Once in deeper waters, they watched dolphins play a game of tag and the shadow of an enormous whale lumber past.

It finally dawned on Ford that his girlfriend was stalling. "What is really going on with you here on the island?" He came up behind her while she was leaning over the railing and trailed his fingers lightly down her side.

She jumped and squealed, whirling around. "Ford! You can't do that. I'm so ticklish, I'll go into massive contortions and fall right over the side of the boat."

His woman was ticklish? Wow, but his day had just gotten a thousand times better! "Fall right over, huh? Just like this?" He swiftly hooked his arms beneath her and hoisted her entire body atop the railing.

She gasped and clung to him. "Don't even think about it!" She gave a nervous laugh as she glanced over her shoulder to the water below. "There are probably sharks down there."

"Then you better start talking, love." He had his arms banded securely around her waist, so there was no real danger of her falling. For the sheer fun of it, he bent her back a few more inches over the rail. That, and so she'd wrap herself more tightly around him.

"You wouldn't!" she taunted.

"I'm still waiting for you to explain yourself." He tipped her a few inches further still. "The film crew. Paisley..."

"It's part of your birthday surprise." She glanced over her shoulder again. "For crying out loud, Ford! I am not a Christmas gift. You can shake me all you want or toss me clean over, and all you'll end up with is a girlfriend turned into seafood for some marine monster."

He tugged her back upright and tumbled her against his chest. "Lucky for you, I'm the only monster you need to worry about."

"Not arguing that fact." She pretended to scowl at him.

"It's partly your fault for looking so hot in your swimsuit." She was wearing her signature white, this time in the form of a halter top with a flippy little skirt.

She blushed and tipped her head against his shoulder again. "As much as I enjoy flirting with the ship's captain, I think it's about time to head back."

"For what?"

She laughed. "You are so not going to weasel it out of me, mister, so give it up."

"Never." He drew her in for one last, very thorough kiss before returning to the wheel where he set a reckless pace back to the island, just so his woman had a reason to keep her arms wrapped around him. He cut his speed as they approached the docks. Once he had the rig idling against the pier, one of the marina attendants took over and secured it for them.

He and Thea walked with their arms slung around each other's waists to the main resort building. As they neared the entrance leading to the elevators, he debated on stealing another kiss before they parted ways.

She smiled at him. "Okay, birthday boy. This is the part where you shower and suit up for your big night."

He pretended to scowl in surprise. "Suit? Nobody said anything about packing a suit."

Her eyes widened. "Please tell me you're joking."

"I'm joking." He'd packed both a suit and a tux.

"So not funny."

"If I had forgotten my suit, would you ditch the formal part of the evening and go back out on the water with me?"

"No. You'd just have to join us inside the ballroom in your board shorts."

He curled his upper lip. "Thanks for the suggestion. I might have to try that sometime."

"Fine. Just not tonight, please. Paisley is..." With a gasp, Thea clapped her hand over her mouth.

"Paisley is what?" The elevator doors rolled open.

"Stop fishing," she protested.

"Make me." To his delight and amusement, she indulged him in an elevator kiss that made him wish more than ever that they could skip whatever was supposed to happen in the ballroom and head back out to the beach.

But the doors rolled open, and she gave him a gentle nudge toward his suite. It was another full hour before he saw her again. This time, she was in a white, heavily sequined cocktail dress.

"You take my breath away, beautiful."

"Sweet!" To his annoyance, the door to the suite he was sharing with Elon reopened at just the wrong moment. His friend appeared in a black suit, much like his own. "Let's hyperventilate our way to the ballroom together, shall we?" As they headed down the hall together, he slapped a hand over his chest, pretending surprise. "Oh, wait. My bad. I just realized you weren't talking to me. You were trying to have a Romeo moment back there, weren't you?"

Since they were in semi-formal attire, Ford resisted the urge to slug his friend or throw him over one of the railings into the nearest water feature.

The door to the room Thea was sharing with Eloise opened a moment later, and her friend joined them in a gold dress that caught the lights and flashed with each move she made.

"Here." Elon smirked at him. "We'll show you how it's done." He tugged his goddess of a fiancée over his arm for a very showy kiss.

"If he goes missing in a few days," Ford growled, steering a chuckling Thea around the two of them, "don't go looking. I was planning on dropping him off in the ocean on our way back to the States."

They reached the ballroom to find the lights were turned down low. However, there were enough sconces low-lit on the back walls to see that Roman and Celine had arrived ahead of them.

"Why's it so dark in here?" Ford drew Thea closer. "Not that I'm complaining."

"Because of this." She lightly clapped her hands, and a single spotlight flashed on in the center of the room.

It illuminated Paisley, who was suspended from a double set of her red and green Christmas silks. She looked a bit like a snow bunny in a lacy white dress with flowers threaded through her hair.

"Happy birthday, daddy!" she called to him. Then she held out a hand. "Come dance with me."

He glanced down at Thea in dawning wonder, finally understanding. She'd managed to uncover one of his deepest, longest-standing yearnings — a wish that no magic or medicine on earth had been able to grant him, so far — a dance with his daughter.

"Go on!" Thea cried in a stage whisper. "You should never keep a lady waiting."

Beneath the rolling cameras, Ford strode to the center of the ballroom floor to meet the most precious little girl in the world beneath the spotlight. Somewhere in the distance, a quartet strummed the opening notes of a lilting, waltz-worthy version of Happy Birthday.

Paisley, bless her sweet heart, used her silks to keep herself upright as they swayed back and forth together. After a moment, he gave her an experimental twirl. She tipped her head back and laughed in giddy delight.

And Ford danced with his daughter for the first time.

He didn't care how odd it might look to their audience that he was dancing with a redheaded girl who was held up by silks. Or how blurred his vision grew. Or how damp his face got. He cuddled the sweet form of his miracle child close until the end of the song.

Then it was time for a surprise of his own. He'd been waiting for the perfect moment, and this was most definitely it.

"Are you ready, sugar?" he inquired softly of his dance partner.

Paisley nodded happily. "All ready, daddy!"

Together, they beckoned for Thea to join them in the center of the room. After a moment of hesitation, she glided in their direction. His vision blurred again with emotion, making a trick of the lights form a halo-like glow around her white-blonde hair. By the time he blinked, she was standing in front of him, close enough for him to see the tracks of dampness running down her own cheeks.

Gazing at her with his heart in his eyes, he took a knee before her, but he let Paisley do the talking.

Her sweet, high-pitched voice rang out. "Will you marry my daddy and become my new mommy?"

Thea's eyes glowed and then misted. "Yes." She held out her arms to them.

Ford stood to gather his two very special ladies close to his heart. "My family," he declared softly.

"And mine," Thea echoed.

EPILOGUE

THEA

One year later

"Merry Christmas, Texas!" Thea's voice rang out from the massive television screen inside Ford's cozy home theater. She and Paisley were cuddled in the oversized black lounge chairs on either side of Ford. Well, Paisley had started out in her own chair, anyway. She was now perched on Ford's knee, happily pointing at the screen.

"That's me and my mama!" she cried, pausing to clap her hands. She never got tired of watching her debut into television. Neither did Thea or Ford.

His fingers, which were threaded through hers, tightened as they reached the part at the end where he'd enjoyed his first-ever father-daughter dance. No, not quite the end of the show, actually. The very last part was Paisley's proposal for Thea to marry her daddy and become her mommy.

Which she now was.

"I love you, Ford," she said softly and was rewarded when he leaned closer to nuzzle her cheek.

"I love you, too, sweetheart. Forever and always." His voice was caressing, and the look he gave her promised that he'd follow it up with a real kiss once Paisley was tucked into bed.

"You say that a lot," Paisley noted idly.

"I love you, too, Paisley," Thea chuckled. "I say that a lot, too, because I mean it a lot."

"Are you going to say it to the baby when he gets here?"

"Of course I will." Thea's hand drifted to her blooming belly.

"But you'll still say it to me?" Paisley's smile slipped and her voice was now laced with suspicion.

"I will always say it to you, my precious girl, because I will always love you." Thea gave Paisley a moment to process that bit of information, knowing it was normal for an only child to feel a little jealous about the pending arrival of a sibling.

When Paisley finally glanced up, frowning, Thea sought to steer the subject to safer ground. "Why do you always call the baby a he?" She reached over to lightly tug one of Paisley's pert little braids. "It could be a baby sister, you know."

"No!" the child stormed, looking petulant. "You already have a girl, so it *has* to be a boy."

Ah. Her fears ran even deeper than Thea had imagined. She glanced over at Ford, looking for help.

He shrugged and bounced the child on his knee a few times, then reached up to tickle her beneath her chin.

She giggled, momentarily distracted.

Then his expression sobered. "Because of you, princess, your mama and I happen to think little girls are pretty magical, so we wouldn't be at all disappointed if the baby turns out to be another girl."

At her splutter of protest, he gave a *tsk-tsk* and tapped her nose. "Regardless of whether you end up with a baby sister or a baby brother, though, the fact remains that you will always be the big sister." He tapped her nose a second time. "The one and only big sister in our family."

"Oh." Her frown relaxed to something a little less ferocious. "I guess you're right."

"And speaking of big sisters, this one," he pointed at her chin, "happens to have a birthday coming up soon. Is there something new on your wishlist that you'd like your mama and me to know about?"

"We-e-e-ll." She glanced up at the ceiling, as if thinking particularly hard. "I've already been on T.V., I already have a new mama, I almost have a new baby, and I've been to Fiji."

"Sheesh! Rough life, kid," Thea muttered.

"What else is left?" In her short, nearly seven years, the child had already ridden in limousines, yachts, private jets, a horse-drawn carriage, and even a submarine.

Paisley's expression cleared, as a thought struck her. "The moon," she noted in satisfaction. "That's where I want to go next." Her lips twisted into a perfect pout as she swiveled in her daddy's arms. "Remember the book you read me about rocket launches last night?"

It was Ford's turn to look to Thea for help.

"Sorry, captain." She pointed at her belly. "Busy incubating a baby here. You may have to work on launching our little artist into space all by yourself."

"Maybe we should wait until the baby is born," Paisley added hastily, glancing between her parents. "I wouldn't want to leave him behind."

"Saved by the baby," Thea chuckled. "Looks like you'll have a few more months to build your rocket ship, Ford."

"Yeah, well, you're the one who taught me anything is possible." Covering Paisley's eyes, he lowered his head to hers and stole a quick but thorough kiss. "We'll figure something out. We always do."

Paisley squirmed and giggled. "Are you kissing again?"

"I sure am. And my next kiss is going to go right

about...here." He dove in to plant a raspberry on her belly.

As their combined laughter filled the room, Thea closed her eyes, reveling in the happiness that only comes from family and home.

Like this book? Leave a review now!

Have you read all three of my billionaire birthday romance stories? In case you missed one, here they are:
The Billionaire's Birthday Date
The Billionaire's Birthday Blind Date
The Billionaire's Birthday Secret

*Looking for your next sweet billionaire romance series? Check out **Her Billionaire Boss**, book #1 in the Amazon bestselling **Black Tie Billionaires Series** — and be swept away by another swoon-worthy hero billionaire CEO.*

Much love,
Jo

SNEAK PREVIEW: HER BILLIONAIRE BOSS

Jacey Maddox didn't bother straightening her navy pencil skirt or smoothing her hand over the sleek lines of her creamy silk blouse. She already knew she looked her best. She knew her makeup was flawless, each dash of color accentuating her sun kissed skin and classical features. She knew this, because she'd spent way too many of her twenty-five years facing the paparazzi; and after her trust fund had run dry, posing for an occasional glossy centerfold — something she wasn't entirely proud of.

Unfortunately, not one drop of that experience lent her any confidence as she mounted the cold, marble stairs of Genesis & Sons. It towered more than twenty stories over the Alaskan Gulf waters, a stalwart high-rise of white and gray stone with tinted windows, a fortress that housed one of the world's most brilliant think tanks. For generations, the sons of Genesis had ridden the cutting edge of industrial design, developing the concepts behind some of the nation's most profitable inventions, products, and manufacturing processes.

It was the one place on earth Jacey was least welcome.

Not just because of how many of her escapades had hit the presses during her rebel teen years. Not just because she'd possessed the audacity to marry their youngest son against their wishes. Not just because she had encouraged him to pursue his dreams instead of their hallowed corporate mission — a decision that had ultimately gotten him killed. No. The biggest reason Genesis & Sons hated her was because of her last name. The one piece of herself she'd refused to give up when she'd married Easton Calcagni.

Maddox.

The name might as well have been stamped across her forehead like the mark of the beast, as she moved into the crosshairs of their first security camera. It flashed an intermittent red warning light and gave a low electronic whirring sound as it swiveled to direct its lens on her.

Her palms grew damp and her breathing quickened as she stepped into the entry foyer of her family's greatest corporate rival.

Recessed mahogany panels lined the walls above

a mosaic tiled floor, and an intricately carved booth anchored the center of the room. A woman with silver hair waving past her shoulders lowered her reading glasses to dangle from a pearlized chain. "May I help you?"

Jacey's heartbeat stuttered and resumed at a much faster pace. The woman was no ordinary receptionist. Her arresting blue gaze and porcelain features had graced the tabloids for years. She was Waverly, matriarch of the Calcagni family, grand-mother to the three surviving Calcagni brothers. She was the one who'd voiced the greatest protests to Easton's elopement. She'd also wept in silence throughout his interment into the family mausoleum, while Jacey had stood at the edge of their gathering, dry-eyed and numb of soul behind a lacy veil.

The funeral had taken place exactly two months earlier.

"I have a one o'clock appointment with Mr. Luca Calcagni."

Waverly's gaze narrowed to twin icy points. "Not just any appointment, Ms. Maddox. You are here for an interview, I believe?"

Time to don her boxing gloves. "Yes." She could feel the veins pulsing through her temples now. She'd prepared for a rigorous cross-examination but had not expected it to begin in the entry foyer.

"Why are you really here?"

Five simple words, yet they carried the force of a

full frontal attack. Beneath the myriad of accusations shooting from Waverly's eyes, Jacey wanted to spin on her peep-toe stiletto pumps and run. Instead, she focused on regulating her breathing. It was a fair question. Her late husband's laughing face swam before her, both taunting and encouraging, as her mind ran over all the responses she'd rehearsed. None of them seemed adequate.

"I'm here because of Easton." It was the truth stripped of every excuse. She was here to atone for her debt to the family she'd wronged.

Pain lanced through the aging woman's gaze, twisting her fine-boned features with lines. Raw fury followed. "Do you want something from us, Ms. Maddox?" Condescension infused her drawling alto.

Not what you're thinking, that's for sure. I'm no gold-digger. "Yes. Very much. I want a job at Genesis." She could never restore Easton to his family, but she would offer herself in his place. She would spend the rest of her career serving their company in whatever capacity they would permit. It was the penance she'd chosen for herself.

The muscles around Waverly's mouth tightened a few degrees more. "Why not return to DRAW Corporation? To your own family?"

She refused to drop the elder woman's gaze as she absorbed each question, knowing they were shot like bullets to shatter her resolve, to remind her how unwelcome her presence was. She'd expected no other reception from the Calcagni dynasty; some would even argue she deserved this woman's scorn. However, she'd never been easily intimidated, a trait that was at times a strength and other times a curse. "With all due respect, Mrs. Calcagni, this *is* my family now."

Waverly's lips parted as if she would protest. Something akin to fear joined the choleric emotions churning across her countenance. She clamped her lips together, while her chest rose and fell several times. "You may take a seat now." She waved a heavily be-ringed hand to indicate the lounge area to her right. Lips pursed the skin around her mouth into papery creases, as she punched a few buttons on the call panel. "Ms. Maddox has arrived." Her frigid tone transformed each word into ice picks.

Jacey expelled the two painful clumps of air her lungs had been holding prisoner in a silent, drawn-out whoosh as she eased past the reception booth. She'd survived the first round of interrogations, a small triumph that yielded her no satisfaction. She knew the worst was yet to come. Waverly Calcagni was no more than a guard dog; Luca Calcagni was the one they sent into the boxing ring to finish off their opponents.

Luca apparently saw fit to allow her to marinate in her uneasiness past their appointment time. Not a surprise. He had the upper hand today and would do everything in his power to squash her with it. A full hour cranked away on the complicated maze of copper gears and chains on the wall. There was nothing ordinary about the interior of Genesis & Sons. Even their clocks were remarkable feats of architecture.

"Ms. Maddox? Mr. Calcagni is ready to see you."

She had to remind herself to breathe as she stood. At first she could see nothing but Luca's tall silhouette in the shadowed archway leading to the inner sanctum of Genesis & Sons. Then he took a step forward into a beam of sunlight and beckoned her to follow him. She stopped breathing again but somehow forced her feet to move in his direction.

He was everything she remembered and more from their few brief encounters. Much more. Up close, he seemed taller, broader, infinitely more intimidating, and so wickedly gorgeous it made her dizzy. That her parents had labeled him and his brothers as forbidden fruit made them all the more appealing to her during her teen years. It took her fascinated brain less than five seconds to recognize Luca had lost none of his allure.

The blue-black sheen of his hair, clipped short on the sides and longer on top, lent a deceptive innocence that didn't fool her one bit. Nor did the errant lock slipping to his forehead on one side. The expensive weave of his suit and complex twists of his tie far better illustrated his famed unpredictable temperament. His movements were controlled but fluid, bringing to her mind the restless prowl of a panther as she followed him down the hall and into an elevator. It shimmered with mirrored glass and recessed mahogany panels.

They rode in tense silence to the top floor.

Arrogance rolled off Luca Calcagni from his crisply pressed white shirt, to his winking diamond and white gold cuff links, down to his designer leather shoes. In some ways, his arrogance was understandable. He guided the helm of one of the world's most profitable companies, after all. And his eyes! They were as beautiful and dangerous as the rest of him. Tawny with flecks of gold, they regarded her with open contempt as he ushered her from the elevator.

They entered a room surrounded by glass. One wall of windows overlooked the gulf waters. The other three framed varying angles of the Anchorage skyline. Gone was the old-world elegance of the first floor. This room was all Luca. A statement of power in chrome and glass. Sheer contemporary minimalism with no frills.

"Have a seat." It was an order, not an offer. A call to battle.

It was a battle she planned to win. She didn't want to consider the alternative — slinking back to her humble apartment in defeat.

He flicked one darkly tanned hand at the pair of Chinese Chippendale chairs resting before his expansive chrome desk. The chairs were stained black like the heart of their owner. No cushions. They were not designed for comfort, only as a place to park guests whom the CEO did not intend to linger.

Jacey planned to change his mind on that subject before her allotted hour was up. "Thank you." Without hesitation, she took the chair on the right, making no pretense of being in the driver's seat. This was his domain. Given the chance, she planned to mold herself into the indispensable right hand to whoever in the firm he was willing to assign her. On paper, she might not look like she had much to offer, but there was a whole pack of demons driving her. An asset he wouldn't hesitate to exploit once he recognized its unique value. Or so she hoped.

To her surprise, he didn't seat himself behind his executive throne. Instead, he positioned himself between her and his desk, hiking one hip on the edge and folding his arms. It was a deliberate invasion of her personal space with all six feet two of his darkly arresting half-Hispanic features and commanding presence.

Most women would have swooned.

Jacey wasn't most women. She refused to give him the satisfaction of either fidgeting or being the first to break the silence. Silence was a powerful weapon, something she'd learned at the knees of her parents. Prepared to use whatever it took to get what she'd come for, she allowed it to stretch well past the point of politeness.

Luca finally unfolded his arms and reached for the file sitting on the edge of his desk. "I read your application and resume. It didn't take long."

According to her mental tally, the first point belonged to her. She nodded to acknowledge his insult and await the next.

He dangled her file above the trash canister beside his desk and released it. It dropped and settled with a papery flutter.

"I fail to see how singing in nightclubs the past five years qualifies you for any position at Genesis & Sons."

The attack was so predictable she wanted to smile, but didn't dare. Too much was at stake. She'd made the mistake of taunting him with a smile once before. Nine years earlier. Hopefully, he'd long forgotten the ill-advised lark.

Or not. His golden gaze fixed itself with such intensity on her mouth that her insides quaked with uneasiness. Nine years later, he'd become harder and exponentially more ruthless. She'd be wise to remember it.

"Singing is one of art's most beautiful forms," she countered softly. "According to recent studies, scientists believe it releases endorphins and oxytocin while reducing cortisol." *There.* He wasn't the only one who'd been raised in a tank swimming with intellectual minds.

The tightening of his jaw was the only indication her answer had caught him by surprise. Luca was a man of facts and numbers. Her answer couldn't have possibly displeased him, yet his upper lip curled. "If you came to sing for me, Ms. Maddox, I'm all ears."

The smile burgeoning inside her mouth vanished. Every note of music in her had died with her husband. That part of her life was over. "We both know I did not submit my employment application in the hopes of landing a singing audition." She started to rise, a calculated risk. "If you don't have any interest in conducting the interview you agreed to, I'll just excuse my—"

"Have a seat, Ms. Maddox." Her veiled suggestion of his inability to keep his word clearly stung.

She sat.

"Remind me what other qualifications you disclosed on your application. There were so few, they seem to have slipped my mind."

Nothing slipped his mind. She would bet all the money she no longer possessed on it. "A little forgetfulness is understandable, Mr. Calcagni. You're a very busy man."

Her dig hit home. This time the clench of his jaw was more perceptible.

Now that she had his full attention, she plunged on. "My strengths are in behind-the-scenes marketing as well as personal presentations. As you are well aware, I cut my teeth on DRAW Corporation's drafting tables. I'm proficient in an exhaustive list of software programs and a whiz at compiling slides, notes, memes, video clips, animated graphics, and most types of printed materials. My family just this morning offered to return me to my former position in marketing."

"Why would they do that?"

"They hoped to crown me Vice President of Communications in the next year or two. I believe their exact words were *it's my rightful place.*" As much as she tried to mask it, a hint of derision crept into Jacey's voice. There were plenty of employees on her family's staff who were far more qualified and deserving of the promotion.

Luca Calcagni's lynx eyes narrowed to slits. "You speak in the past tense, Ms. Maddox. After recalling what a flight risk you are, I presume your family withdrew their offer?"

It was a slap at her elopement with his brother. She'd figured he'd work his way around to it, eventually. "No." She deliberately bit her lower lip, testing him with another ploy that rarely failed in her dealings with men. "I turned them down."

His gaze locked on her mouth once more. Male interest flashed across his face and was gone. "Why?"

He was primed for the kill. She spread her hands and went for the money shot. "To throw myself at your complete mercy, Mr. Calcagni." The beauty of it was that the trembling in her voice wasn't faked; the request she was about to make was utterly genuine. "As your sister by marriage, I am not here to debate my qualifications or lack of them. I am begging you to give me a job. I need the income. I need to be busy. I'll take whatever position you are willing to offer, so long as it allows me to come to work in this particular building." She whipped her face aside, no longer able to meet his gaze. "Here," she reiterated fiercely, "where *he* doesn't feel as far away as he does outside these walls."

Because of the number of moments it took to compose herself, she missed his initial reaction to her words. When she tipped her face up to his once more, his expression was unreadable.

"Assuming everything you say is true, Ms. Maddox, and you're not simply up to another one of your games," he paused, his tone indicating he thought she was guilty of the latter, "we do not currently have any job openings."

"That's not what your publicist claims, and it's certainly not what you have posted on your website." She dug through her memory to resurrect a segment of the Genesis creed. "Where innovation and vision collide. Where the world's most introspective minds are ever welcome—"

"Believe me, Ms. Maddox, I am familiar with our corporate creed. There is no need to repeat it. Especially since I have already made my decision concerning your employment."

Fear sliced through her. They were only five minutes into her interview, and he was shutting her down. "Mr. Calcagni, I—"

He stopped her with an upraised hand. "You may start your two-week trial in the morning. Eight o'clock sharp."

He was actually offering her a job? Or, in this case, a ticket to the next round? According to her inner points tally, she hadn't yet accumulated enough to win. It didn't feel like a victory, either. She had either failed to read some of his cues, or he was better at hiding them than anyone else she'd ever encountered. She no longer had any idea where they stood with each other in their banter of words, who was winning and who was losing. It made her insides weaken to the consistency of jelly.

"Since we have no vacancies in the vice presidency category," he infused an ocean-sized dose of sarcasm into his words, "you'll be serving as my personal assistant. Like every other position on our payroll, it amounts to long hours, hard work, and no coddling. You're under no obligation to accept my offer, of course."

"I accept." She couldn't contain her smile this time. She didn't understand his game, but she'd achieved what she'd come for. Employment. No matter how humble the position. Sometimes it was best not to overthink things. "Thank you, Mr. Calcagni."

There was no answering warmth in him. "You won't be thanking me tomorrow."

"A risk I will gladly take." She rose to seal her commitment with a handshake and immediately realized her mistake.

Standing brought her nearly flush with her new boss. Close enough to catch a whiff of his aftershave — a woodsy musk with a hint of cobra slithering her way. Every organ in her body suffered a tremor beneath the full blast of his scrutiny.

When his long fingers closed over hers, her insides radiated with the same intrinsic awareness of him she'd experienced nine years ago — the day they first met.

It was a complication she hadn't counted on.

Grab your copy in eBook, paperback, or Kindle Unlimited on Amazon!
Her Billionaire Boss

Complete series — read them all!
Her Billionaire Boss
Her Billionaire Bodyguard
Her Billionaire Secret Admirer
Her Billionaire Best Friend

Her Billionaire Geek
Her Billionaire Double Date
Black Tie Billionaires Box Set #1 (Books 1-3)
Black Tie Billionaires Box Set #2 (Books 4-6)

Much love,
Jo

NOTE FROM JO

Guess what? There's more going on in the lives of the hunky heroes you meet in my stories.

Because...*drum roll*...I have some Bonus Content for

everyone who signs up for my mailing list. From now on, there will be a special bonus content for each new book I write, just for my subscribers. Also, you'll hear about my next new book as soon as it's out (*plus you get a free book in the meantime*). Woohoo!

As always, thank you for reading and loving my books!

JOIN CUPPA JO READERS!

If you're on Facebook, please join my group, Cuppa Jo Readers. Don't miss out on the giveaways + all the sweet and swoony cowboys!

https://www.facebook.com/groups/ CuppaJoReaders

FREE BOOK!

Don't forget to join my mailing list for new releases, freebies, special discounts, and Bonus Content. Plus, you get a FREE sweet romance book for signing up!

https://BookHip.com/JNNHTK

SNEAK PREVIEW: ACCIDENTAL HERO

Matt Romero was single again, and this time he planned to stay that way.

Feeling like the world's biggest fool, he gripped the steering wheel of his white Ford F-150, cruising up the sunny interstate toward Amarillo. He had an interview in the morning, so he was arriving a day early to get the lay of the land. That, and he was anxious to put as many miles as possible between him and his ex.

It was one thing to have allowed himself to become blinded by love. It was another thing entirely to have fallen for the stupidest line in a cheater's handbook.

Cat sitting. I actually allowed her to talk me into cat sitting! Plus, he'd collected his fiancée's mail and carried her latest batch of Amazon deliveries into her condo.

It wasn't that he minded helping out the woman he planned to spend the rest of his life with. What he minded was that she wasn't in New York City on business like she'd claimed. *Nope.* As it turned out, she was nowhere near the Big Apple. It had simply been her cover story for cheating on him, the first lie in a long series of lies.

To make matters worse, she'd recently talked Matt into leaving the Army for her, a decision he'd probably regret for the rest of his life now that she'd broken their engagement and moved on with someone else.

Leaving me single, jobless, and —

The scream of sirens jolted Matt back to the present. A glance in his rearview mirror confirmed his suspicions. He was getting pulled over. *For what?* A scowl down at his speedometer revealed he was cruising at no less than 95 mph. *Whoa!* It was a good twenty miles over the posted speed limit. *Okay, this is bad.* He'd be lucky if he didn't lose his license over this — his fault entirely for driving distracted without his cruise control on. *My day just keeps getting better.*

Slowing and pulling his truck over to the shoulder, he coasted to a stop and waited. And waited. And waited some more. A peek in his side mirror showed the cop was still sitting in his car and talking on his phone.

Oh, come on! Just give me my ticket already.

To stop the pounding between his temples, Matt reached for the red cooler he'd propped on the passenger seat and pulled out a can of soda. He popped the tab and tipped it up to chug down a shot of caffeine. He hadn't slept much the last couple of nights.

Before he could take a second sip, movement in the rearview mirror caught his attention. He watched as the police officer finally opened his door, unfolded his large frame from the front seat of his black SUV, and stood. However, he continued talking on his phone instead of walking Matt's way.

Are you kidding me? Matt swallowed a dry chuckle and took another swig of his soda. It was a good thing he'd hit the road the day before his interview at the Pantex nuclear plant. At the rate his day was going, it might take the rest of the afternoon to collect his speeding ticket.

He'd reached the outskirts of Amarillo, only about twenty to thirty miles from his final destination. The exit sign for Hereford was up ahead. Or the Beef Capital of the World, as the small farm town was often called.

He reached across the dashboard to open his glove compartment and fish out his registration card and proof of insurance. His gut told him there wasn't going to be any talking his way out of this one. As a general rule, men in blue didn't sympathize with folks going twenty miles or more over the speed limit.

Digging for his wallet, he pulled out his driver's license. Out of sheer habit, he reached inside the slot where he normally kept his military ID and found it empty. *Right.* He no longer possessed one, which left him with an oddly empty feeling.

He took another gulp of soda and watched as the officer pocketed his cell phone. *Finally! Guess that means it's time to get this party started.* Matt chunked his soda can into the nearest cup holder and stuck his driver's license, truck registration, and insurance card between two fingers. Hitting an automatic button on the door, he lowered his window a few inches and waited.

The guy strode up to Matt's truck window with a bit of a swagger. His tan Stetson was pulled low over his eyes. "License and registration, soldier."

Guess you noticed the Ranger tab on my license plate. Matt wordlessly poked the requested items through the window opening.

"Any reason you're in such a hurry this morning?" the officer mused curiously as he scanned Matt's identification. He was so tall, he had to stoop to peer through the window. Like Matt, he had a dark tan, brown hair, and a goatee. The two of them could've passed as cousins or something.

"Nothing worth hearing, officer." *My problem. Not yours. Don't want to talk about it.* Matt squinted through the glaring sun to read the guy's name on his tag. *McCarty.*

"That's too bad, because I always have plenty of time to chat when I'm writing up such a hefty tick-et." Officer McCarty's tone was mildly sympathetic, though it was impossible to read his expression behind his sunglasses. "I clocked you going twenty-two miles over the posted limit, Mr. Romero."

Twenty-two miles? Yeah, that's not good. Not good at all. Matt's jaw tightened, and he could feel the veins in his temples throbbing. It looked like he was going to have to share his story, after all. Maybe, just maybe, the trooper would feel so sorry for him that he'd give him a warning instead of a ticket. It was worth a try, anyway. *If nothing else, it'll give you something to laugh about during your next coffee break.*

"Today was supposed to be my wedding day." He spoke through stiff lips, finding a strange sort of relief in confessing that sorry fact to a perfect stranger. Fortunately, they'd never have to see each other again.

"I'm sorry for your loss." Officer McCarty glanced up from Matt's license to give him what felt like a piercing once over. He was probably trying to gauge if he was telling the truth or not.

"Oh, she's still alive," Matt muttered. "Found somebody else, that's all." He gripped the steering wheel and drummed his thumbs against it. *I'm just the poor fool she cheated on.*

He was so done with dating. At the moment, he

couldn't imagine ever again putting his heart on the chopping block of love. *Better to be lonely than to let another person destroy you like that.* She'd taken everything from him that mattered — his pride, his dignity, even his career.

"Ouch," Officer McCarty sighed. "Well, here comes the tough part about my job. Despite your reasons for speeding, you were putting lives at risk. Your own included."

"Can't disagree with that." Matt stared straight ahead, past the small spidery nick in his windshield. He'd gotten hit by a rock earlier while passing a semi tractor trailer. It really hadn't been his day. Or his week. Or his year, for that matter. It didn't mean he was going to grovel, though. He'd tried to appeal to the guy's sympathy and failed. The sooner he gave him his ticket, the sooner they could both be on their way.

A massive dump truck on the oncoming side of the highway abruptly swerved into the narrow, grassy median. It was a few hundred yards away, but the front left tire dipped down, *way* down, making the truck pitch heavily to one side.

"Whoa!" Matt shouted, pointing to get Officer McCarty's attention. "That guy looks like he's in trouble!"

Two vehicles on Matt's side of the road passed him in quick succession — a rusty blue van pulling a fifth wheel and a shiny red Dodge Ram.

When Officer McCarty didn't respond, Matt laid on his horn to warn the two drivers, just as the dump truck started to roll. It was like watching a horror movie in slow motion, knowing something bad was about to happen while being helpless to stop it.

The dump truck slammed onto its side and skidded noisily across Matt's lane. The blue van whipped to the right shoulder in a vain attempt to avoid the collision. Matt winced as the van's bumper caught the hood of the skidding dump truck nearly head on, then jack-knifed into the air.

The driver of the red truck was only a few car lengths behind, jamming so hard on its brakes that it left two dark smoking lines of rubber on the pavement. Seconds later, it careened into the median and flipped on its side. It wasn't immediately clear if the red pickup had collided with any part of the dump truck. However, an ominous swirl of smoke seeped from beneath its hood.

For a split second, Matt and Officer McCarty stared in shock at each other. Then the officer shoved Matt's license and registration back through the opening in the window. "Looks like I've got more important things to do than give you a ticket." He sprinted toward his SUV, leaped inside, and gunned it toward the scene of the accident with his lights flashing and sirens blaring. He only drove a short distance before stopping his vehicle and canting it across both lanes to form a makeshift blockade.

Though Matt was no longer in the military, his defend-and-protect instincts kicked in. There was no telling how long it would take the emergency vehicles to arrive, and he didn't like the way the red pickup was smoking. The driver hadn't climbed out of the cab yet, either, which wasn't a good sign.

Officer McCarty reached the blue van first, probably because it was the closest, and assisted a dazed man from one of the back passenger seats. He led him to the side of the road, helped him get seated on a small incline, then jogged back to help the driver exit the van. Unfortunately, the officer was only one man, and this was much bigger than a one-man job.

Following his gut instincts, Matt disengaged his emergency brake and gunned his way up the shoulder, pausing beside the officer's vehicle. Turning off his motor, he leaped from his truck and jogged across the highway to the red pickup. The motor was still running, and the smoke was rising more thickly now.

Whoever was behind the wheel needed to get out immediately before the thing caught fire or exploded. Matt took a flying leap to hop on top of the cab and crawl to the driver's door. It was locked.

Pounding on the window, he shouted at the driver, "You okay in there?"

There was no answer and no movement. Peering closer, he could make out the unmoving figure of a woman. Blonde, pale, and curled to one side. The only thing holding her in place was the strap of a seatbelt around her waist. A trickle of red ran across one cheek.

Matt's survival training kicked in. Crouching over the side of the truck, he quickly assessed the undamaged windshield and decided it wasn't the best entry point. *Too bad.* Because his only other option was to shower the driver with glass. *Sorry, lady!* Swinging a leg, he jabbed the heel of his boot into the section of window nearest the lock. By some miracle, he managed to pop a fist-sized hole instead of shattering the entire pane.

Reaching inside, he unlocked the door and pulled it open. The next part was a little trickier, since he had to reach down, *way* down, to unbuckle the woman and catch her weight before she fell. It would've been easier if she were conscious and able to follow his instructions.

Guess I'll have to do it without any help. An ominous hiss of steam and smoke from beneath the hood stiffened his resolve and made him move faster.

"Come on, lady," he muttered, releasing her seatbelt and catching her slender frame before she fell. With a grunt of exertion, he hefted her free of the mangled cab. Then he half-slid, half hopped back to the ground with her in his arms. As soon as his boots hit the pavement, he took off at a jog.

She was lighter than he'd been expecting. Her upper arm, that his left hand was cupped around, felt desperately thin despite her baggy pink and plaid shirt. One long, strawberry blonde braid dangled over her shoulder, and a sprinkle of freckles stood out in stark relief against her pale cheeks.

She didn't so much as twitch as he ran with her, telling him that she was still out cold. He hoped it didn't mean she'd hit her head too hard on impact. Visions of traumatic brain injuries and their long list of complications swarmed through his mind, along with the possibility that he might've just finished moving a woman with a broken neck or back. *Please don't let that be the case, Lord.*

He carried her to the far right shoulder and up a grassy knoll where Officer McCarty was depositing the other injured victims. A dry wind gusted, sending a layer of fine dust in their direction. One prickly, rolling tumbleweed followed. On the other side of the knoll was a rocky canyon wall that went straight up, underscoring the fact that there really hadn't been any way for the hapless van and pickup drivers to avoid the collision. They'd literally been trapped between the canyon and oncoming traffic.

An explosion ricocheted through the air, shaking the ground beneath Matt's feet. On pure instinct, he dove for the grass, using his body to shield the woman in his arms. He used one hand to cradle her head against his chest and his other hand to break their fall as best he could.

A few of the other injured drivers and passengers cried out in fear as smoke billowed around them and blanketed the scene. For the next few minutes, it was difficult to see much, though the wave of ensuing heat had a suffocating feel to it. The woman beneath Matt remained motionless, though he thought he heard her mumble something at one point. He continued to crouch over her, keeping her head cradled beneath his hand. He rubbed his thumb beneath her nose and determined she was still breathing. However, she remained unconscious. He debated what to do next.

A fire engine howled in the distance, making his shoulders slump in relief. Help had finally arrived. More sirens blared, and the area was soon crawling with fire engines, ambulances, and paramedics with stretchers. One walked determinedly in his direction.

"Hi! My name is Star, and I'm here to help you. What's your name, sir?" the EMT worker inquired in a calm, even tone. Her chin-length dark hair was blowing nearly sideways in the wind. She shook her head to knock it away, revealing a pair of snapping dark eyes swimming with concern.

"I'm Sergeant Matt Romero," he informed her out of sheer habit. *Well, maybe no longer the sergeant part.* "Don't worry about me. I'm fine. This woman is not. I don't know her name. She was unconscious when I pulled her out of her truck."

As the curvy EMT stepped closer, Matt could read her name tag. *Corrigan.* "Like I said, I'm here to do everything I can to help." Her forehead wrinkled in alarm as she caught sight of the injured woman's face. "Omigosh! Bree?" Tossing her red medical bag on the ground, she slid to her knees beside the two of them. "Oh, Bree, honey!" she sighed, reaching for her pulse.

"I-I..." The woman stirred. Her lashes fluttered a few times against her cheeks. Then they snapped open, revealing two pools of the deepest blue Matt had ever seen. Though glazed with pain, her gaze latched anxiously onto him. "Don't leave me," she pleaded with a hitch in her voice.

There was something oddly personal about the request. Though he was sure they'd never met before, she spoke as if she recognized him. Her confusion tugged at every one of his heartstrings, making him long to grant her request.

"I won't," he promised huskily, hardly knowing what he was saying. In that moment, he probably would have said anything to make the desperate look in her eyes go away.

"I'm not liking her heart rate." Star produced a penlight and flipped it on. Shining it in one of her friend's eyes, then the other, she cried urgently, "Bree? It's me, Star. Can you tell me what happened, hon?"

A shiver worked its way through Bree's too-thin frame. "Don't leave me," she whispered again to Matt, before her eyelids fluttered closed. Another shiver worked its way through her, despite the fact that she was no longer conscious.

"She's going into shock." Star glanced worriedly over her shoulder. "Need a stretcher over here," she called sharply. One was swiftly rolled their way.

Matt helped the EMT lift and deposit their precious burden on it.

"Can you make it to the hospital?" Star asked as he helped push the stretcher toward the nearest ambulance. "Bree seemed pretty insistent about you sticking around."

Matt's eyebrows shot upward in surprise. He hadn't been expecting yet another person he'd never met before to ask him to stick around. "Uh, sure." In her delirium, the injured woman had probably mistaken him for someone else. However, he didn't mind helping out. *Who knows?* Maybe he could give the attending physician some information about her rescue that might prove useful in her treatment.

Or maybe he was just drawn to the fragile-looking Bree for reasons he couldn't explain. Whatever the case, Matt suddenly wasn't feeling in a terrible hurry to hit the road again. Fortunately, he had plenty of extra time built into his schedule before his interview tomorrow. The only real task he had left for the day was finding a hotel room once he reached Amarillo.

"I just need to let Officer McCarty know I'm leaving the scene of the accident." Matt shook his head sheepishly. "I kinda hate to admit this, but he had me pulled over for speeding before everything went down here." He waved a hand at the carnage around them. It was a dismal scene, punctuated by twisted metal and scorched pavement. All three mangled vehicles looked like they were totaled.

Star snickered, then seemed to catch herself. "Sorry. That was inappropriate laughter. Very inappropriate laughter."

He shrugged, not the least bit offended. A lot of people laughed when they were nervous or upset, which Star clearly had been since the moment she'd discovered the unconscious woman was a friend. "It was pretty stupid of me to be driving these long, empty stretches of highway without my cruise control on." Especially with the way he'd been brooding non-stop for the past seventy-two hours.

Star shot him a sympathetic look. "Believe me, I'm not judging. Far from it." She reached out to pat Officer McCarty's arm as they passed by him with the stretcher. "The only reason a bunch of us in Hereford don't have a lot more points on our licenses is because we grew up with this sweet guy."

"Oh, no! Is that Bree?" Officer McCarty groaned. He pulled his sunglasses down to take a closer look over the top of his lenses. His stoic expression was gone. In its place was one etched with worry. The personal kind. Like Star, he knew the victim.

"Yeah." Star's pink glossy lips twisted. "She and her brother can't catch a break, can they?"

Since two more paramedics converged on them to help lift Bree's stretcher into the ambulance, Matt paused to face the trooper who'd pulled him over.

"Any issues with me following them to the hospital, officer? Star asked me if I would." Unfortunately, it would give the guy more time and opportunity to ticket Matt, but that couldn't be helped.

"Emmitt," Officer McCarty corrected. "The name is Emmitt, alright? I think you more than worked off your ticket back there."

Sucking in a breath of relief, Matt held out a hand. "Thanks, man. I really appreciate it." It was a huge concession. The guy could've taken his license if he'd wanted to.

They soberly shook hands, eyeing each other.

"You need me to come by the PD to file a witness report or anything before I boogie out of town this evening?" Matt pressed.

"Nah. Just give me a call, and we'll take care of it over the phone." Emmitt produced a business card and handed it over. "Not sure if we'll need your story, since I saw it go down, but we should probably still cross every T."

"Roger that." Matt stuffed the card in the back pocket of his jeans.

"Where are you headed, anyway?"

"Amarillo. Got an interview at Pantex tomorrow."

"Nice! It's a solid company." Emmitt nodded. "I've got several friends who work there."

Star leaned out from the back of the ambulance. "You coming or what?" she called impatiently to Matt.

He nodded vigorously. "I'll follow you," he called back and jogged back to his truck. Since the ambulance was on the opposite side of the highway, he turned on his blinker and put his oversized tires to good use while traversing the median. He had to spin his wheels a bit in the center of the median to get his tires to grab the sandy incline leading to the other side. He was grateful all over again that he'd splurged on a few upgrades for his truck to make it fit for off-roading.

He followed the ambulance north and found himself driving the final twenty minutes or so to Amarillo, probably because it boasted a much bigger hospital than any of the smaller surrounding towns — more than one, actually. Due to another vehicle leaving the parking lot as he was entering it, Matt was able to grab a decently close parking spot. He jogged into the waiting room, dropped Star Corrigan's name a few times, and tried to make it sound like he was a close friend of the patient.

Looking doubtful, the receptionist made him wait while she paged Star, who appeared a short time later to escort him into the emergency room. "Bree's in Bay 6," she informed him in a strained voice, reaching for his arm and practically dragging him behind the curtain.

If anything, Bree looked even thinner and more fragile than she had outside on the highway. A nurse was stooped over her, inserting an I.V. into her arm.

"She still hasn't woken up." Star's voice was soft, barely above a whisper. "They're pretty sure she has a concussion. Sounds like they're gonna run a full battery of tests to figure out what's going on."

Matt nodded, not knowing what to say.

The lovely EMT's pager went off. She snatched it up and scowled at it. "I just got another call. It's a busy day out there for motorists." She texted a message on her cell phone, then cast him a sideways glance. "Any chance you'll be able to stick around until Bree's brother gets here?"

That's when it hit Matt that this had been the EMT's real goal all along — to ensure that her friend wasn't left alone. She'd known she could get called away to the next job at any second.

"Not a problem." He offered what he hoped was a reassuring smile. Amarillo was where he'd been heading, so he'd already reached his final destination. "I wasn't planning on going far, anyway. Got an interview at Pantex in the morning."

"No kidding! Well, good luck with that," she

returned with a curious, searching look. "A lot of my friends moved up this way for jobs after high school."

Officer Emmitt McCarty had said something similar. "Hey, ah..." Matt hated detaining the EMT any longer than necessary, but it might not hurt to know a few more details about the unconscious woman, since he was about to be alone with her. "Mind telling me Bree's last name?"

"Anderson. Her brother is Brody. Brody Anderson. They run a ranch about halfway between here and Hereford, so it'll take him a good twenty to thirty minutes to get here."

"It's alright. I can stay. It was nice meeting you, by the way." His gaze landed on Bree's left hand, which was resting limply atop the white blankets on her bed. She wasn't wearing a wedding ring. *Not that it matters. I'm a complete idiot for looking.* He forced his gaze back to the EMT. "Sorry about the circumstances, of course."

"Me, too." She shot another worried look at her friend and dropped her voice conspiratorially. "Hey, you're really not supposed to be back here since you're not family, but I sorta begged and they sorta agreed to overlook the rules until Brody gets here." She eyed him worriedly.

"Don't worry." He could tell she hated the necessity of leaving. "I'll stick around until her brother gets here, even if I get booted out to the waiting room with the regular Joes."

"Thanks! Really." She whipped out her cell phone. "Here's my number in case you need to reach me for anything."

Wow! Matt had not been expecting the beautiful EMT to offer him her phone number. Not that he was complaining. It was a boost to his sorely damaged ego. He dug for his phone. "I'm ready when you're ready."

She rattled off her number, and he quickly texted her back so she would have his.

"Take care of her for me, will you, Matt?" she pleaded anxiously.

On second thought, there was nothing flirtatious about Star's demeanor. It was entirely possible that their exchange of phone numbers was exactly what she'd claimed it was — a means of staying in touch about the status of her friend's condition. Giving her a reassuring look, Matt fist-bumped her.

Looking grateful, she pushed aside the curtain and was gone. The nurse followed, presumably to report Bree's vitals to the doctor on duty.

Matt moved to the foot of the hospital bed. "So, who do you think I am, Bree?" *And why did you beg me not to leave you?*

Her long blonde lashes remained motionless against her cheeks. It looked like he was going to have to stick around for a while if he wanted answers.

Accidental Hero
Available in eBook and paperback on Amazon +
FREE in Kindle Unlimited!

Read them all!
A - Accidental Hero
B - Best Friend Hero
C - Celebrity Hero
D - Damaged Hero
E - Enemies to Hero
F - Forbidden Hero
G - Guardian Hero
H - Hunk and Hero
I - Instantly Her Hero
J - Jilted Hero
K - Kissable Hero
L - Long Distance Hero
M - Mistaken Hero
N - Not Good Enough Hero
O - Opposites Attract Hero

Much love,
Jo

ALSO BY JO GRAFFORD

For the most up-to-date printable list of my books:

Click here

or go to:

https://www.JoGrafford.com/books

For the most up-to-date printable list of books by Jo Grafford, writing as Jovie Grace (*sweet historical romance*):

Click here

or go to:

https://www.jografford.com/joviegracebooks

ABOUT JO

Jo is an Amazon bestselling author of sweet and inspirational romance stories about faith, hope, love and family drama with a few Texas-sized detours into comedy. She also writes sweet and inspirational historical romance as Jovie Grace.

1.) Follow on Amazon!
amazon.com/author/jografford

2.) Join Cuppa Jo Readers!
https://www.facebook.com/groups/
CuppaJoReaders

3.) Follow on Bookbub!
https://www.bookbub.com/authors/jo-grafford

4.) Follow on YouTube
https://www.youtube.com/channel/
UC3R1at97Qso6BXiBIxCjQ5w

amazon.com/authors/jo-grafford

bookbub.com/authors/jo-grafford

facebook.com/jografford